HORSE AND DOG STORIES

Edited by Charlotte Fyfe

CAVALIER PAPERBACKS

Published 1995 by Cavalier Paperbacks

PO Box 1821

Warminster

Wilts BA12 OYD

ISBN 1-899470-05-0

Typeset by John Leighton Designs

Printed and bound by The Guernsey Press Company Limited

ACKNOWLEDGEMENTS

The Publishers wish to thank the following for permission to use copyright material in this collection:

Christine Pullein-Thompson for the extract from Phantom Horse © (1955); Josephine Pullein-Thompson for A Horribly Horsey Daughter © (1979); Monica Edwards for Sure Magic.

While every effort has been made to obtain permission, there may still be cases in which we have failed to trace a copyright holder, and we would like to apologise for any apparent negligence.

CONTENTS

HORSE
AND DOG STORIES

PHANTOM HORSE An Extract
Christine Pullein-Thompson

Jean and her brother are living in the US. When they hear of a beautiful wild Palomino living in the mountains, they are determined to catch him. But he always evades them, until one day Jean sets out alone to find him.

I knew at once that it was Boxing Day. I rushed to the window and saw that the snow outside was crisp and knew that there had been frost. I dressed quickly in my sky-blue jersey and jodhpurs. Outside the air was sharp; the snow crunched under my feet. The bay mare heard the back door slam and whinnied. I felt as though I was setting out on a tremendous expedition, as I mixed her feed. I might have been about to climb Everest. It was that sort of morning.

I sang as I boiled a kettle in the kitchen. I rushed upstairs with tea for everyone.

"You're shooting today," I told Angus, because he can't remember things early in the morning, and I knew he would be furious if he slept till ten o'clock by mistake.

Dad said, "Why so early?"

I couldn't stop to explain. I felt in a tremendous hurry. I wanted to be riding alone in the mountains seeking the wild horse. "It's a quarter past eight," I answered, as I left the room and rushed downstairs.

I mucked out the bay mare's box in ten minutes. Then I started to make toast for breakfast.

"What's the hurry?" Angus asked, appearing yawning in the kitchen. "It's not you who's shooting."

"I know. But I'm going to find the wild horse," I answered. "He may be starving."

"What, in this weather? Do you think you'll be allowed to go?" Angus asked. He sounded as though he didn't think it likely.

"I'm going, whatever anybody says. We can't leave him to starve. It's cruelty to animals," I replied.

1

"Be careful we don't shoot you. Anyway, I don't believe he's around here at all. Everybody thinks he's moved on," Angus said.

"Well, I'm just going to make sure," I replied. "And now look what you've made me do," I cried, as the kettle boiled all over the stove.

"It's nothing to do with me. You've simply filled it too full," Angus said.

I felt all on edge, and now I was terrified that my parents would forbid an expedition into the mountains.

"Why don't you come shooting? Wendy is," Angus said.

"No thank you. I don't feel like killing things," I replied. "Do you think Mum and Dad are ever coming down? Do you think we can start without them?" I asked.

"Why don't you get breakfast and then get going before anyone comes down to say no? That's what I would do," Angus said.

I knew that it was a bad suggestion. But I couldn't bear the thought of not going. "Won't you get the blame then? I don't want you to be stopped shooting," I answered, making coffee.

"That doesn't matter. It's your expedition which matters," my brother said. "Here, you go," he added, seizing a jug out of my hand. "I'll make the coffee."

I said, "Thanks terribly," and I snatched a hunk of bread and spread it with butter, and rushed out to the stable munching. I filled my pockets with nuts and fetched a halter and the bay mare's tack.

Two minutes later I was mounting in the yard. "Good luck," Angus called softly from the back door. I shouted, "thank you," and "goodbye," but he had already returned to the kitchen. I hoped he wouldn't talk. I trotted briskly across the sparkling snow, feeling as though I belonged to the distant past, before the advent of cars and the machine age.

The Hereford cattle were clustered around the Millers' farm waiting to be fed. Ground hogs and deer had left prints in the snow. The valley seemed empty and quite devoid of sound. It wasn't the valley I knew any more - just a vast white wilderness.

The trail leading into the mountains looked smaller and quite different beneath the snow. The coated trees had thawed a little before they froze, so that now weird, fantastic icicles encased their branches like thick glass. The bay mare's hoofs made fresh prints in the snow and it was obvious she and I were the first beings to tread the trail since Christmas night. There was the tiniest breeze which faintly stirred the encrusted leaves and made the trees creak uneasily; otherwise there was no sound and we might have been travelling through a dead world.

I thought of my parents eating breakfast at home; cracking the tops of boiled eggs, spreading toast with butter and marmalade. I hoped they weren't too angry at my behaviour; for though I was certain that I was on an errand of mercy, I was afraid they wouldn't see my expedition in the same light.

It was hard work following the trail; soon the bay mare was sweating and I was watching her ears to avoid the glare from the snow. I came to a fork and turned left for no particular reason. Here deer had left tracks in the virgin snow. My hands were cold in my smart new gloves and my feet were cold inside my shoes. The sky had turned a miraculous blue, the sort of blue which belongs to the Riviera and the South of France. The sun was melting the snow where it reached the tree tops. It was the sort of day and setting one dreams about.

I don't know how long I rode nor how far before I saw the first hoofprints in the snow, and knew that my hunch was right and that somewhere not far away the wild horse walked alone through the mountains. I began to feel excited then, because I knew that my journey was justified and that there was hope again on the horizon. I hurried the bay mare and I think she knew that we were near our goal, for she seemed to take new heart.

Soon I heard the distant sound of firing and, in my

3

imagination, I saw the Millers and Angus ploughing through the snow with guns. Then the hoofprints left the trail and we were plodding through undergrowth and under trees and over half-buried rocks. I think the bay mare could smell the Palomino, for she seemed to follow the hoofprints with great eagerness and once or twice she stopped to smell the air.

I started to wonder what would happen when the wild horse saw us. I dreaded an exciting chase. Where the snow was melting beneath the sun it formed into hard balls in the bay mare's hoofs and several times she stumbled and almost fell. Once she seemed to be walking on stilts, and I was about to dismount when the ball fell out and lay a dirty grey lump on the white snow.

I had been lost for some time when we reached a tiny clearing and saw, standing alone beneath a tree, a horse coated with snow and ice. It was the Palomino, but he looked quite different. He seemed half asleep and icicles hung from his mane and fetlocks; his ribs showed through the snow on his sides; and his eyes were partly closed and dull as though life didn't interest him any more. In spite of his awful appearance, my heart gave a leap of joy, for at least I had found him, at least he was still alive.

He raised his head a little as we approached, and the bay mare whinnied softly. A tattered headcollar hung on his tired head. I'd never seen a horse look so weary before. I was nearly crying as I dismounted from the bay mare. I felt no triumph at all.

I said, "Hello, whoa, little horse," as I approached the Palomino, and though his tired eyes watched me warily, he didn't move. I knew then that he was very sick. I reached out a hand and took the piece of rope which dangled from his headcollar and still he didn't move. I saw that his eyes were almost yellow and so were his nostrils and his mouth. I wondered then whether he was strong enough to journey home. I tied the halter I had brought on to his headcollar and brushed the snow off his thin, drooping neck. The bay mare rubbed her head against him, but he gave no response.

He wouldn't eat the nuts out of my pockets. I rubbed his cold, half-frozen ears and I could feel him falling to sleep again. I knew then that somehow I had to get him home and that he would never stand another night in the mountains. I guessed that he had come to the clearing in the small hours and that he hadn't moved since; it looked as though it had been his home for some time.

I stood and wished that I had Angus with me and that I was in England and could reach a telephone in a few minutes and summon a horse-box. I wished that Pete was with me because I was sure he would know how to handle the situation. I felt very helpless alone in the mountains with the two horses. My hands were numb and snow from the few thawing trees had dripped down my neck. At that moment I hated Virginia and the Blue Ridge Mountains more than anywhere else in the world. I hated the icicles and the snow and the endless trails which all looked just alike. I hated the sky and the sun and the remoteness and the few birds now hovering in the air looking for dying animals to eat.

Wendy had told me once about these birds. She called them an omen of death; and now they were just above, cawing greedily – a hungry flock of birds waiting for the Palomino to die.

I knew I couldn't leave the Palomino to seek help when I saw the birds. I was frightened that they would swoop while I was away and when I returned I would find only a heap of newly picked bones. I had heard that these birds didn't wait for animals to die, only until they were too weak to fight any more, then they descended and the mountains echoed with the screams of the dying animal.

The birds made up my mind for me. I pulled gently on the halter and said, "Come on phantom horse, we're going home." He looked like a phantom covered with snow – a phantom ghost on his last pilgrimage.

The bay mare encouraged him with another whinny. I think she knew how ill he was. At last my words and the pull on his headcollar seemed to reach his brain; he moved with awkward stiff steps as though his limbs were frozen. He was so pitiful that I cried and my tears made little holes in the snow. I had to go back the way I had come because it was the only way I knew.

I followed the bay mare's hoofprints back through the undergrowth, under the trees and over the rocks. Every few minutes I had to stop and let the Palomino rest. It was ages before I reached the trail again.

And then I saw that the weather had changed. The sun had gone. The sky was no longer blue, but the sort of grey which means snow. The air was much warmer; and I knew that I had to hurry because soon there would be fresh snow which would obliterate the hoofprints and then I would be really lost. Already the snow was soft on the trail. I sunk in a foot each time I took a step and my jodhpurs were soon soaking right up to the knee. I walked between the two horses and the bay mare hurried and the Palomino lagged; it wasn't a pleasant journey.

And then the snow came in large, white flakes. It fell on my hair, on the horses, on the trail and the trees and undergrowth, it fell as though it would never stop falling.

I thought of the time then, of my parents waiting anxiously at home. I began to wonder whether I should ever reach the warmth and safety of Mountain Farm while it was still possible. Nobody was shooting any more. The mountains were wrapped in silence except for the shifty, eerie sound of falling snow; all prints had vanished, nothing seemed to live except myself and the two horses.

I started to wish that I had brought provisions. My tummy told me that it was lunch time; my legs felt weak and I longed for a bar of chocolate or a large ham sandwich. I tried to heighten my morale by imagining the Palomino in the stable at home, but when I looked at him and saw his utter weariness I started to wonder whether he would live if we ever did reach home.

I shall never forget the next few hours. We plodded on and on and the trail looked just the same. And the bay mare started to tire and to look back as though we had taken the wrong turning and were now walking directly away from home. And I began to worry, I saw night falling, the snow deepening. I wondered whether my parents would send out a search party. I felt terribly guilty and for a moment I wished I hadn't listened to Angus's advice in the morning; then I looked at the Palomino again and suddenly I didn't regret anything any more. It was so wonderful to think that if he lived he would really be ours.

I thought of hunting across a russet and gold Virginian countryside, of seeing him from my window early in the morning and knowing that he was ours, of feeding him late at night and riding him in the spring. I saw us jumping in shows, competing in hunter trials, bringing home a red rosette. I saw myself rounding up cattle on him with Phil and Pete, schooling him in the paddock at home. I saw him wearing elegant rugs with our initials in one corner. I plodded on through the snow lost in my own happy imagination, ceasing to notice my aching legs, the feeling of afternoon, or the falling, endless snow.

Dusk came quite suddenly, it came with a darkening sky and a whispering evening breeze. I had followed the same trail for hours, yet nothing seemed changed. Both horses were dragging by this time, and I'm sure they knew I was lost. When I halted, the Palomino stood drearily with hanging head, and a sickly eye which showed no interest at all in anything. I looked down the trail and, reasoning that we must reach somewhere some time, I plodded on. The wind blew the snow in our faces and my eyes started to run, and my gloves were wet from where the snow had melted when it met the warmth of my hands. I started to sing to raise my spirits. I sang songs from American musicals and "Tipperary." Then I began singing hymns.

Because of the snow, night came without darkness. And then, quite suddenly, I saw twinkling lights shining through the trees.

I started to hurry then and I shouted to the horses, "Come on. We're getting somewhere at last." But they wouldn't hurry; they had lost all confidence in me; they dragged and the snow balled more and more in their hoofs, and they stumbled and jerked my arms, while I pulled frantically on the rope and the reins, losing all sense and reason in a wild desire to reach the twinkling lights.

Then I thought of shouting. "I'm coming. Is there anyone about? I've caught the wild horse," I called and my voice echoed and came back muffled by the sound of falling snow.

I hurried on and gradually the lights seemed nearer. The snow was very deep now and soft and wet, so that it was hard work moving at all.

And then I thought I heard an answering call, and I started to shout twice as loud. "It's Jean. I'm all right. I've got the wild horse," I yelled over and over again.

Soon I could feel a stronger breeze blowing through the trees and, quite suddenly, there was more light and space, and we had reached a valley, and with a cry of joy, I saw that it was our valley.

I tried to run and fell sprawling in the snow. The horses waited patiently until I was on my feet again; and the bay mare raised her head and looked across the valley to where the lights shone bravely in Mountain Farm.

I remember hoping that there would be someone at home when I arrived. I was terrified lest the whole district should be out searching for me. And now I saw that there were lots of little lights moving about the valley. There were tiresome little gusts of snow, and drifts. I started to shout, "I'm coming, I'm coming, I'm coming," until the words were all jumbled together and didn't make sense any more.

The bay mare was hurrying too now. She jogged and bumped the Palomino and he stumbled and almost fell. I slackened my pace then. I didn't want to take a dead horse home.

I talked to the Palomino. "Soon you'll be in a lovely warm stable, a really super one," I told him. "There'll be lots to eat and gradually you'll get well again."

I stopped and patted him and rubbed his ears and he stood with his legs sprawled apart as though he couldn't move another step. If it had been possible to get a horse-box to him I think I would have left him there, but as it was I had to keep him moving.

Then I thought I heard a shout and I started to call again and someone called, "It's Jean. She's reached the valley." After that there was a great deal of shouting and suddenly a bell rang out loud and clear, drowning the voices and the sound of falling snow. Lights seemed to be moving towards me from all directions and the bay mare was dragging me faster and faster towards Mountain Farm, and somewhere behind me, the Palomino was dragging on my other arm until I thought it must fall from its socket. And I kept yelling, "It's Jean. I'm home," till someone said quite close, "It's all right now, we know," and I saw my brother and beyond him the back door standing open.

"I've got the wild horse," I said. "But he's terribly ill. I think we should have the vet at once. He's almost dead. That's why I've been so long." I started to cry then, because the Palomino really did look ill, and I was suddenly sure that he wouldn't last more than a few hours, because his eyes looked sunken in their sockets and he was hardly breathing any more.

"Let's get him inside," Angus said.

"Where are Mum and Dad?" I asked.

"Looking for you," Angus replied, taking the bay mare. "It's all right. They will have heard the bell; that was to be the signal."

"You mean that I was home?" I asked, and Angus nodded.

The Palomino tottered into the empty loose-box. He seemed in a coma. I don't think he had any idea where he was.

I shut the box door. "I'll ring up the vet," I said. I felt I must do it immediately, before my parents arrived and I had to explain.

I asked the exchange to put me through to the nearest vet and the girl who answered said, "Will Doctor Beecher do?"

I almost replied, "No, I want a vet not a doctor," before I remembered that vets are called doctors in America. "Sure, fine," I answered.

I saw that the snow on my clothes was melting in pools on the hall floor. Then Dr Beecher answered and I told him what had happened, speaking as slowly and coherently as I could. When I had finished speaking, he said, "Okay, I'll be right over," and hung up. I thought of him hurrying for his coat, starting his car. Then I began to wonder whether he would ever reach us on such a night.

Angus had settled the bay mare when I returned to the stable. She had piles of straw under her rugs and was munching a hot feed.

"I had it all ready," he said. "But I don't know what to do about the Palomino. He won't eat a thing."

"He's terribly ill. Have you noticed how yellow he is?" I asked.

"Let's hope the vet can do something," my brother replied.

"Hello, are you there, Jean?" someone called, and I saw my parents wading through the snow.

"Yes, I'm back. I've got the wild horse. He's very ill. I think he's dying. That's why I've been so long."

I was afraid they would be angry. But Dad said, "We thought it was something like that."

And Mum said, "If only you would choose better weather for your expeditions. But perhaps now you've got the wretched horse, you'll stop giving us frights."

"I'm terribly sorry. I didn't mean to stay out so long," I replied.

"It doesn't matter," Mum answered.

There were more voices now and Pete and Phil and Wendy

came into the yard.

"Congratulations, Jean," Pete said, taking my hand.

"He's terribly ill," I replied quickly. "He may die." I didn't want congratulations. I didn't think bringing a sick horse home was a deed which deserved congratulations – it's something you do expecting no reward, I thought, besides, no one with a heart could have left the Palomino to die in the mountains.

"I've rung up the vet. He's coming right over," I said.

"You'd better come in and change. You look soaked," Mum said.

"What about the Palomino? He shouldn't be left alone," I cried.

"We'll look after him," Dad answered. "Hurry up and have a hot bath and get some food inside you. Then we can talk."

I went indoors with Mum and she pulled off my wet jodhpurs and I suddenly discovered that I was terribly tired and ravenously hungry.

I ate some bread and butter and had a hot bath and changed. There was hot soup waiting for me in the kitchen and braised ham and potatoes.

Angus was leaning against the stove. "The vet hasn't come yet. I've sent the Millers home," he told me. "Wendy would talk and the Palomino needs quiet."

"I thought they were going to New York," I replied.

"The weather's stopped them. The road's blocked near Baltimore," Angus said.

"Did you have a good shoot?" I asked, remembering the morning which seemed so long ago. "No, the snow was too deep. We hardly killed anything. By the way, I told Mum and Dad that you probably wouldn't be back to lunch. That's why they didn't start worrying till tea time."

I looked at the clock and saw that it was six o'clock. I had imagined that it was nearly supper time.

"Were they furious?" I asked.

"They were rather," Angus answered. "They said that you

were going mad over the wild horse."

Mum and Dad came in from the stables.

"He does look in a bad way. I think I'll ring up Smythe. He'd better know we've got his horse," Dad told us.

"Jean's horse now," Angus replied.

"Yours too. Because if it hadn't been for you I wouldn't have gone," I told Angus.

It was ages before Dr Beecher came. We had all eaten supper by that time taking it in turns to watch the Palomino. Dad had talked to Mr Smythe for hours on the telephone, and we knew now that if the Palomino lived he would be ours for ever and ever.

At last, there was a knock on the back door and a small man stood in the yard clutching a black bag.

"I'm real sorry I've been so long. I've walked the last three miles, the road's blocked by a ten foot wall of snow," he said.

I liked Dr Beecher at once. We all hurried to the stable where Angus was watching the Palomino. The vet didn't talk much.

He murmured, "Gee, he's bad. He's eaten something really bad." Then he mentioned poison and jaundice and found the Palomino had a temperature of a hundred and five. He gave him three injections and stood and looked at him for some time.

"There's nothing more we can do tonight but hope," he said at last. "I'll stop by first thing tomorrow."

"Are you sure you wouldn't like to stay the night?" Mum asked.

"Thank you Ma'am. I guess I'd better not. Maybe I'll get some more calls tonight," Dr Beecher replied.

It was very quiet when Dr Beecher had left.

"Well, that's that. We can do no more," Dad said.

"What were the injections?" Angus asked. "Penicillin, iron and liver - or some sort of food or vitamins - I don't know what the other one was," Dad replied.

"He's bringing some sort of drench in the morning," Mum

said.

We looked at the Palomino before we went to bed. He was lying down and he looked happier, though still terribly ill.

"Do you think he will live?" I asked Dad.

"Who can tell? We can only hope, as Dr Beecher said," Dad replied.

I hated going to bed. Outside the snow was still falling. It seemed sad to have caught the wild horse at last and not to know whether he would live or die. Not that I cared very much whose horse he was - I only wanted him to live.

I prayed for the Palomino before I fell asleep. I remember Angus coming into my room and saying, "If he lives, let's call him Phantom, because he looked like a phantom coming across the valley with you tonight, all covered with snow and thin and out of another world."

"All right," I answered. "If he lives."

And now everything is nearly told. For the Palomino lived; after three days of hovering between life and death, he stood on his legs again and looked over his loose-box door.

As Angus suggested, we named him Phantom, and perhaps because of our English accents or perhaps because we rescued him, he seems to love Mountain Farm and whinnies when he sees us, and is much loved by us all.

As I write this I can see his head looking over his box door. He's fat and shining now and his flaxen mane hangs tidily on the right side of his gleaming, golden neck.

Since Phantom came to live with us, Angus and I have become much nicer and far more sensible. We don't get lost any more because Phantom always knows the way home; and we don't lose our heads, because now he's ours, there doesn't seem anything worth pursuing through the ever-changing Blue Ridge Mountains of Virginia.

THE MYSTERIOUS MOUNTAIN DOG
Mary Gilchrist

Down the driveway leading between the green lawns strolled the town-dog one morning, and he did not stop until he had reached the gate. Arriving there, he planted his four legs firmly apart and glared around. Such a beautiful scene lay before him it was hard to believe that even a dog could be angry on such a morning. Before him just beyond the roadway, lay a little loch as calm as a gleaming mirror, reflecting the swans that sailed upon it. On one side of the loch there were bushes of yellow broom and beyond the loch and the farther roadway there was a stretch of moorland, while high in the purple background loomed a mountain. This was the mountain which annoyed the town-dog, for somewhere in its vicinity lived the mountain-dog.

Now it so happened that Gyp, the town-dog, had been brought to the beautiful place by his master on holiday.

Every morning, when you awakened, you rushed outdoors to begin a joyful day. There was the roadway to explore and the grass to roll in, and sometimes you were taken for country walks. Last night, however, Gyp had been enjoying himself on the lovely hill of bracken that rose like a baby mountain behind the house.

Well, after Gyp had rolled in the bracken until he was quite tired, he decided to walk to the gate before going to bed.

"I'm the happiest dog in the world," he said as he looked around, and he raised his voice in a happy bark. Scarcely had the sound of it quivered across the loch than "Wouff!" came a great loud voice from beyond the mountain. At the sound of it Gyp stopped on his way up the path; he was so astonished that any dog should dare to answer him. "Wouff, wouff, wouff!" he yelped fiercely, as if to say, "Did anyone dare to bark at me?" and "Wouff, wouff, wouff!" came distinctly over the hill in reply.

"Well I never!" growled Gyp to himself, and was so angry that the hair on his neck stood up like a fan. So there he stood and barked and barked far into the evening, while the mountain-dog barked back as though determined to get the last word.

Thus it happened on this fine morning that Gyp took up his stand at the gate, with legs planted firmly apart, and prepared to tell the mountain-dog what he thought of him. Just as he was about to give a dreadful bark, he noticed his good friend Bonzo strolling along.

"Hello, Bonzo," he greeted, wagging his stumpy tail. "I say, did you hear me barking a lot last night?"

"I should think I did," snorted Bonzo, looking severely at Gyp.

Now Bonzo, besides being young and handsome, was, Gyp knew, a very good-natured dog; so that if he was annoyed by the barking it must have been bad indeed.

"What were you barking about?" inquired Bonzo.

Whereat Gyp the town-dog told Bonzo the whole story of how he had barked with happiness and a mountain-dog mocked at him.

"Good gracious! What impudence!" sympathised Bonzo. "I should just like to find him; shouldn't you?" said he.

"Why, that's a good idea," agreed Gyp. Just then there was a scurrying noise in the roadway and the sound of excited sniffs, and a little black dog named Waggles came jumping along.

"Good morning, Waggles," said Gyp and Bonzo.

"Did you hear old Gyp barking last night?" asked Bonzo.

"Yes," panted Waggles, "and I distinctly heard a mountain-dog answer him."

At this, Gyp looked at Bonzo as if to say, "I told you so!"

Well, the three of them put their heads together. There was no doubt about it, he ought to be found and punished, no matter how big or fierce he was.

"I'll teach him not to anger me," muttered Gyp.

"I'll bite him if he bites you," said Bonzo.

"I'll run for a police-dog to help you," offered Waggles.

"Let's start off at once," pleaded Bonzo eagerly, and without more fuss, off they set along the loch road as fast as they could run.

Soon they had turned the corner and passed the other side, where the ducks were diving under the water for food. Next they arrived on the great, broad highway, but soon, much to Gyp's relief, they turned in from the hard road, and passed through a gateway on to a private path. Bonzo knew the way quite well: he had often been there before, but he never knew that it led to the mountain-dog. It was the prettiest road that you could imagine, and it wound like a twisted ribbon that had lost the end of itself amongst the hills.

"Ha! Ha!" chuckled Waggles, who was enjoying himself hugely, "Won't that smart old dog get a scare when we arrive!"

So on they trotted, on past tiny hills carpeted with heather, amongst which wound a little path all zigzag with great rough boulders and small white pebbles. This pathway was really the bed of a stream, which in winter filled up with rain and became a river. On the other side was a copse of trees with a border of yellow whin, with blossoms like tiny lanterns hanging from the branches. Presently they reached a wood, and there the three lay down for a rest.

High overhead, the great trees swayed and rustled and seemed to whisper, as though the passing wind had told them some news. A few old trees had a wrapping of moss that wound around their trunks, like old old men with rugs around their knees. On the ground, beneath the hanging branches, there lay a carpet of grass, with patches of coloured wild flowers here and there. Pink and red and blue they were, and tender baby ferns that shyly hid their heads against the trees. The loveliest flowers of all, however, were the bluey-mauve wild hyacinths that covered all the ground within the wood. They looked so frail and sweet and cool, with their crisp tall leaves of green that seemed to guard the fragile blooms from harm. Hundreds and hundreds and hundreds there were, waving amongst the trees, in exquisite shades of pink and blue and mauve.

Suddenly in the midst of this deep and dream-like silence, a bunny rabbit popped up amongst the ferns!

At this very moment Waggles, who was almost asleep, caught sight of its bobbing tail, and his black eyes glowed and sparkled with excitement. "Yap! Yap!" he yelped, jumping up wide awake, "There goes a rabbit!" and off he scampered after it.

Down through the hyacinths he scurried, and along the bank of a stream; deeper and deeper into the wood, while bunny raced on in front.

It all happened so suddenly that poor Gyp and Bonzo, who had been almost asleep too, sat up and blinked. "You were asleep!" they teased each other, and gave themselves a shake, but not a sign of the naughty Waggles could be seen. "Waggles, come here!" they growled and shouted, but not a sound could they hear.

"Oh well," sighed Bonzo, "it can't be helped, we shall go on without him," so he and Gyp went on their way through the wood.

Suddenly, between the trees beyond the little stream, they saw the truant Waggles standing still. His ears were both cocked up, as if he was doing his best to catch a sound.

"Here we are, here we are!" yelped both Gyp and Bonzo, and immediately they heard the strangest sound.

From over the mountain beyond the wood it wafted quite distinctly, the mocking voice of the mountain-dog, crying "Here we are!"

Poor Gyp and Bonzo were so astonished that they stood as if turned to stone, and they even forgot to scold Waggles.

"Did you hear that?" whispered Bonzo at last. Gyp's hair stood on end with anger. "Come on, you two, let's hurry," he growled, "we have delayed too long," and on they rushed again faster than ever.

They ran so fast that poor Waggles was panting, with his tongue hanging out of his mouth, for he had used up his rest time in chasing the rabbit. On went Gyp, although he was old and his knees somewhat stiff; but he was so anxious to fight the mountain-dog that he did not feel them.

"Wouff! wouff!" came back over the hills.

You may be sure that this last insult made them madder than ever, and they all ground their teeth when they thought of that mountain-dog. Gyp was quite sure that the brute was black, with ugly, red, gleaming eyes, so no wonder he wanted both Bonzo and Waggles to help him.

On they ran, while the mountain where the dog lived seemed as distant as ever. At last they felt that they could run no longer, so down they flopped side by side on the grass that grew by an old stone wall.

"If only we could catch a glimpse of him we would soon scare him to death," wailed poor Bonzo, who was tired and thirsty. Waggles, too, was weary and worn; he was tenderly licking his paws, while poor old Gyp was kept awake only by his anger.

"I'll tell you what," announced Bonzo at last, struck by a happy thought, "let's all bark together and see if he is still there."

So gathering up all their strength and breath, they gave a terrific howl.

"Good gracious! What on earth was that noise?" asked the farmer's startled wife, and she rushed to one of the little windows to look out.

Lying in the shade near the farmhouse door, with his nose on his paws and his eyes on the distant hills, lay Rover the sheep-dog, who also heard the howl. He sat up quickly and looked around to where the ducks and hens were, but it was evident that there was nothing the matter with them. Then up he jumped, looking quite grim with his dark brown shaggy coat as he strolled down the path. Now, as you know, there are many

18

large dogs who, although they look very fierce, show by their kind soft eyes that they are really nice. Thus it was that when Bonzo and Gyp and Waggles saw him coming, they were not afraid but greeted him with wagging tails.

"Good day, my friends," he grunted in a very deep soft voice, "I just came out to see who gave that howl."

At this, the three dogs all started talking at once, trying to explain to Rover, about the great mountain-dog who persisted in insulting them and whom they meant to punish.

"He mocks at me for days and nights and makes me dreadfully angry," said Gyp.

"He jeered at us in the wood today!" yapped Waggles excitedly, and "Just let me get at him!" snorted Bonzo. Well, when old Rover heard all about it, he did the oddest thing; he sat down and laughed! He laughed so hard that his sides were aching and tears came into his eyes, as though it was the best joke he had ever heard. Bonzo and Gyp and Waggles were naturally angry, to be laughed at like this, but they guessed that old Rover was wise, so they stared at each other in a puzzled way. At last old Rover recovered himself and invited them into the farmyard, where they ate what was left of his dinner, and drank from the pond.

"Now," said Rover, seating himself beside the other three, "you must forgive me for laughing at you just now; you have been cheated all the time."

"Cheated?" growled Gyp. "What do you mean? Who has been cheating us?"

"You have come all this way in search of an echo!" said Rover.

He then explained to the astounded dogs that he too used to be angry when his every bark was mocked by the mountain-dog. By and by, however, as he grew older and became a clever sheep-dog, the farmer took him out amongst the hills.

"Now," he thought, "I will find that dog and ask him what he means."

Over the purple mountains he looked, and down in the sleepy valley, but never a single mountain-dog did he see. Yet always when he raised his voice and rent the clear, still air, faintly from far away came the same bark. So the clever sheep-dog had reasoned it out with himself, and concluded that there was no mountain-dog but only an echo. For always, no matter how loudly he barked or how high, how quick or how slow, the voice that answered was always the very same.

Poor Gyp felt very stupid when he heard this explanation, but the others saw the joke, and soon they were all three laughing at themselves. When at last they bade kind Rover goodbye, they promised to call again, and bring him all the news from the village.

SURE MAGIC

Monica Edwards

"When I were eleven I didn't have thirty pounds in my money-box nor did I have one." Old Tim Terrell leaned on his spade for a moment and got his breath while looking at Paul reflectively.

"I've been saving for two years," Paul pointed out. "But now I almost think I shall have to give up," he added sadly. "It's funny, but when I started I thought I'd only have to save very hard and carefully, and I'd soon have enough to buy a pony. But, of course, I was very young then."

Old Tim took a whetstone out of his pocket, upended his spade and began sharpening the edge of it. "Thass a thing I wholly do believe in," he said, "an edge to a spade." He suddenly looked up again for a moment, the whetstone poised.

"You could get yourself a real nice nanny goat with that. Chap what sold me mine, he got another up for sale, I do know. Now thass a useful animal, is a nanny goat. Usefuller than riding a pony would be, I will say. All that milk. Your Mum'd be pleased, I lay."

"But I don't what a goat."

"Ah well, that do make a difference," the old man admitted, resuming the digging, which he was doing for Paul's father. And then he added persistently: "Some folks do drive 'em in a liddle cart, and that."

"What I'm in two minds about," said Paul, "is spending it on a second-hand air-gun. Roy Boley's got one at Partridge Farm that he said I could have for twenty pounds. I thought I'd go and look at it this afternoon. Of course I'd much rather have a pony, even if it meant waiting another two or three years, but I'd only have sixty or seventy pounds then, at this rate. It's pretty hopeless, isn't it, Tim?"

Mr Terrell looked at his watch and then he looked at the heavy sky. "Thass full of snow," he said, "for all it's near the end of March. If you are to go out to Partridge and back, I lay you better start now. That'll get dark early, see, with all that cloud, and your Mum'll worry."

"If I had a pony," Paul said, "I'd be there and back in no time, galloping across the fields."

"If wishes was horses," said Tim Terrell, "beggars would ride. Now mind my pea-rows - troddlin' all over 'em." He glanced up again at a sky that looked like suspended London fog and shook his head. "I tell you, spring ain't what it used to be, no it ain't. I call to mind when I were a tiddler -" But Paul, apologetically waving his hand, was already out of earshot.

Partridge Farm had several attractions for Paul, the air-gun being one of the least. For one thing, there was Roy; a good friend and wonderful company on ferreting expeditions, though quite incredibly disinterested in horses. Oh, the waste of it, Paul thought as he strode across the fields: here was a boy whose father kept and rode such a splendid hunter mare as Calluna was, a boy who could have kept a pony of his own if he had wanted to, but who was much more interested in the two farm tractors and the cowman's motor cycle.

A further attraction for Paul was the Ayrshire dairy herd. He liked to help in the cowsheds when he could, and Roy often joined him there, though with him the tractors always took first place. But the greatest attraction of all at Partridge was Calluna, and Mr Boley had a special liking for Paul because of this. He would dearly have liked his own son, Roy, to share his interest in horses and hunting, but failing this it was nice to have Paul about the stable, being useful and absorbed in all that happened there.

Calluna was shortly expecting a foal and so had not been hunted through the winter just finished. The sire was a very premium stallion and Calluna herself was an excellent type of hunter mare, so that Paul and Mr Boley expected great things of the foal. In about a fortnight it would be born. Feeling snow suddenly brush his cheeks, Paul wondered what sort of a world it would be born to. Winter, with east winds and snow? Or spring, with mild sunshine? Anything, it seemed, could happen in an English spring. This time last year they had been picnicking. Now it looked as if they might be sledging in the morning.

Once started, the snow began to fall fast, like plum petals in a sudden wind, and by the time Paul reached the farm the ground was white. They were already milking in the long cow-shed, but Paul stopped to look over the loose box at Calluna, talking to her and offering her the quartered apple he had brought for her. But she was restless, staring past him at the snow and then walking round her box and staring out again. She took the apple politely but crunched it as if her mind was not on it.

"I expect it does look odd to you, old girl," said Paul, rubbing his hands down the old corduroy shorts that he wore in school holidays, "when you thought it was spring." And he went across to the cow-shed, shaking the snow from his hair as he hurried inside.

It was the usual thing that, whenever Roy and Paul were at each other's houses around a meal-time, they stayed there for it, unless it was going to be dark before they could get home again. "And tonight, even with the snowy sky, it ought to be light till half-past six," Mr Boley said.

"And there's cherry cake for tea," said Roy, "and we can look at the air-gun after."

But somehow, they never did look at the air-gun. At tea the talk turned to Calluna and her great expectations, and Paul mentioned how restless she had seemed when he had looked in at her.

"That's the snow, I daresay," said Mr Boley. "We haven't had much this winter, for all it's been so cold, and I expect it looked strange to her, coming down so fast and swirly. Anyway, we'll have a look at her after tea, and I always go round last thing, too. You never know with mares in foal, though really she ought to go another fortnight."

"What I'm wondering about," said Mrs Boley, glancing

through the window a little anxiously, "is Paul getting home safely. I wonder if you ought to start early, Paul? I don't want to hurry you, but it does seem to be getting thicker."

"It is jolly thick," said Roy. "You can't even see where the path is any more."

"Oh, I'll be all right," said Paul. "It can't be really deep before I get home, and I can go back by the road."

"Tell you what," said Mr Boley; "we'll go out and have a look at the old girl, shall we, and then I'll see you back as far as the signpost?"

Mr Boley's hands were deep in his pockets as they trudged through the snow to the stable. "It's already up to the ankles," he said. "Pity the poor wretches who have their dairy herds lying out!"

Because their heads were tucked down against the blizzard they did not notice the open stable door until they were nearly in front of it. Then, for a moment, they stood staring in horrified disbelief at the empty loose box. Mr Boley swung round, peering through the snow into the corners of the yard. "She can't be far off," he muttered in a shocked voice, adding as if to himself, "in this weather, and growing dusk, and so near to foaling. Did you notice if the door was properly shut when you looked in at her, Paul?" They were hurrying across to the cow-shed now.

"It seemed quite firm when I leaned on it," panted Paul, hurrying too. "How on earth could she have got out?"

"Heaven only knows," said Mr Boley, staring into the shadows of the cow-shed. But Calluna wasn't there, and the double row of white-splashed cows looked up curiously, clanking their chains. "She used to be a bit of a devil at getting out when she was younger," he added. "Used to pull the bolt back with her lips. But we thought she'd grown out of that, these three years past."

"How about tracks?" Paul asked anxiously, peering now at the snowy ground.

"No, it's falling too thick for that, son. You can hardly see our own tracks from the house. We'll have to send out searchers. With lanterns, too; it'll be dark in an hour. But I'll get out the car and run you to the signpost before I join them."

"Oh – couldn't I help to look for Calluna?" Paul's voice went up in an urgent appeal. "You could telephone Mother: she wouldn't mind, I'm sure. I could get back all right if you lent me a torch." "Sorry, old chap." Mr Boley looked at him regretfully. "I couldn't have the responsibility. Job enough finding the mare, I daresay – it may take us all night, in this – without keeping an eye on chaps of Roy's and your age. Come along to the house for a minute while I get the search started, and then I'll soon have you on the road. You can come straight out again in the morning," he added, seeing Paul's forlorn face. "But we want grown men on this job."

The next ten minutes for Mr Boley were a whirl of telephoning, and sending one person to fetch another, and someone else to search the farm buildings, until he was satisfied that four were about to set out seeking Calluna, and that the police were on the look-out as well. Roy brought out the air-gun, to fill up the time usefully, but Paul hardly felt so interested in it now. He kept looking up, out of the dusky window where snowflakes flew before the wind, and imagining Calluna out in it, probably foaling in it; because, as Mr Boley said, you never knew with mares in foal.

That night the snow fell heavily until dawn. The telegraph wires were down in many places, so that, when Paul got up in the morning, he could not get through to Partridge Farm to inquire about the search. But news came very quickly, of its own accord, on the legs of old Tim Terrell. Tim was postman as well as jobbing gardener in Paul's village, and he stood on the doorstep stamping his feet and sorting letters while Paul looked out past him at the amazing snow of spring. "Treating you well, this morning," Tim was saying. "Five letters, and not a bill among them."

"Have you heard anything about the Boleys' search party, Tim?"

"I have that. Just been talking to the chap what's driving the snow-plough, and he says their cowman told him as they found the mare in Merlin Wood." He was talking through the fingers of a glove that he held in his mouth while handling letters.

"Oh, I am glad they found her!" cried Paul, taking the letters. "Was she all right?"

"Right enough," said Tim, "but what do you think? With a foal at foot! In all that snow."

"Tim! Really? Is the foal all right, too? Oh, Mr Boley will be pleased!"

"The little 'un's good as new, he say," said Tim. "Funny, ain't it, the things they'll stand? Sometimes you hear of 'em digging out sheep what have been buried days and days in them deep hill drifts. I reckon they got air and warmth down in that snow – must have, mustn't they? Oh well, this won't do." Mr Terrell swung his bag round his back again and then set off on his way.

Paul would have thrown his coat and gumboots on and trudged to Partridge Farm at once, if his mother hadn't reminded him that he had not made his bed or dried the breakfast things, which were his holiday tasks, but he was out there before the morning was half over. He found Mr Boley in the loose box with Calluna and there, walking experimentally about in the straw on long stilty legs, was the most beautiful but quite the tiniest colt he had ever seen.

"Oh I say!" Paul stared in rapturous awe. "Isn't he small?"

"Fortnight premature, of course," said Mr Boley. "Lucky to find him when we did. It was close on dawn; we'd been trudging all the countryside. No tracks, you see, until the snow began to clear. Still, he seems well enough for all his bitter welcome. It's his mother that worries me."

"She looks all right to me," said Paul, studying her anxiously.

"Won't settle," said Mr Boley. "She doesn't seem to care about the little fellow at all. Seems to want to get out in the snow again. Look at her fretting! I can't make it out. I've been trying to get her to stand for feeding him, off and on, ever since we brought her in. But you can see for yourself how it is."

Paul could see very easily now, for Calluna fussed around her box with her swinging stride, throwing her head up at the doorway and staring out over the snow with strange restless eyes. And this was the way she went on behaving through all of that day. Paul stayed for lunch, but not for tea because of the snow, and most of his time he spent with Mr Boley in Calluna's box, trying to get the mare to settle quietly with her foal.

"She's always been such a good mother before," the farmer said in a baffled voice. "And this little chap – he's so small, being premature, he wants a good start. I don't reckon he's had a proper meal yet. Now, see if she'll stand quietly while you hold her, and I'll help with the colt."

But Calluna swung her quarters this way and that, and stared out at the snow as if it were a green summer meadow and she was starving.

The next morning, with the snow still deep on the ground and no birds singing, Paul went to the door in answer to Tim Terrell's knock. "Mouldy old lot I brought you this morning," said Tim, who always took a great interest in the letters. "Four circulars and a postcard."

"How's Calluna, Tim? Have you seen her this morning? Has she settled down yet, do you know?"

"Cor! That's a case, that is," said Tim, shaking his head. "Rumbusting around her box all night, whinnying and that, so Mr Boley says. Don't know what to do with her, they don't, and that's a fact, 'cept padlock her door. Nice little tiddler too, the colt. But she don't seem to take to him at all. Just fussing to get out."

"Oh Tim!" Paul stared at the letters without seeing them. "How awful for the colt. I wish – oh, I wish that he were my colt! I think he's quite the loveliest thing I ever saw. So small, and yet so – sort of perfect."

"You wouldn't be able to ride him now, not for years," Tim pointed out, straightening his shoulders under the heavy bag.

"I know. But it isn't only riding that's such fun. It's having a horse, and being able to look after it, and all that."

"Tell you what, then," said Mr Terrell helpfully. "You want to find out where the old mare dropped her foal, son; then go there and wish, see. Sure magic, that is – to wish where a foal's been newly born. But he must be a colt foal, mind, or it doesn't work out." "This one is," said Paul, his eyes suddenly lighting up with interest. But in a moment they had darkened again. "Magic and all that, isn't really true of course," he said wistfully.

"Tell you what parson said in the pulpit, Sunday – since you was at home with your cold –" said Tim Terrell. "He said: 'There's more things in heaven and earth than this world dreams of'. Well, this won't do; I must be getting along down the lane now. Cheerybye, son. So-long."

Paul took the letters in and shut the door. He made his bed and dried the breakfast things, and then fetched in some logs for the sitting room fire. Then he put on his wellies and coat and set off for Partridge Farm.

Merlin Wood, wasn't it, where Calluna's foal had been born? It lay between Paul's house and the farm, as near as mattered. At a pinch, he might say it was almost on his way. Of course, no one believed in magic these days, but all the same, it wouldn't do any harm just to trudge about inside the wood for a bit. No one need know, least of all Roy Boley, who was exceedingly practical with his carburettors and magnetos and overhead drive and the like – good chap though he was.

The snow on the edges of the wood was thicker than in the fields. It reached nearly to the top of Paul's wellies in places, and drifts of it were so deep that he had quickly to step out of them, though none had fallen since the night of Calluna's escape. Paul saw her tracks here and there, in sheltered places, and the tracks of men. Some of the prints were half-hidden by the snow that had fallen during the search, some stopped and turned back, and others were criss-crossed and lost in muddle. Trudging through deep drifts, Paul began to think he would never find the place. And for how long could one still consider the colt 'newly born,' as Tim had said he must be? Nearly a day and a half had passed already ...

Suddenly Paul stared, opening his eyes wider, hurrying faster though the snow lipped into his boot-tops. Here, many tracks came together; the snow was trampled, pawed and scattered. Hoof-prints and shoe-prints overlapped - and there, sure enough, was the smoothed hollow in the snow where the mare had lain down. Paul stopped, puffing from his struggle through the drifts and flushed with the cold damp of snowy woods. This was the place. Here was where the small colt had first opened his eyes; not to daylight but to clouded star-light.

Oh well, Paul decided to himself in an offhand manner, now that he was here he might as well make a wish. After all, anything could happen, especially in a wood called Merlin ...

He never could be certain, afterwards, whether he had, in fact, wished at all before, suddenly, he saw two small brown leaf-things sticking up from the snow. Like leaves, they were, but not quite leaves, and they stood in the top of drift against the hedge, not ten yards away. He could almost imagine that one of them had moved. Then something seemed to pull tight in Paul's chest as he floundered forward. He bent and scrabbled at the snow with wet-gloved hands; the small leaf-brown things shook and flickered under his eyes, and - really, yes, there was no doubt whatever about it, but - impossible thought it might seem - he knew he was looking at the damp dark ears of a newborn foal.

Gently now, but tense with horrified anxiety, the gloved hands scraped and swept and felt their way. And under them the curled form of the foal was gradually revealed. It looked at

29

him with vague, heavy-lidded eyes, snuffling a little at the snow around it's nostrils and shivering at the sudden cold air on wet skin. It was alive - a twin foal of Calluna's! Buried in the snow for a day and a half and still alive - though smaller, even, than the little one already at the farm.

Thinking quickly, Paul pulled off his coat and bent to rub the wet furry coat with the sleeves of it. He rubbed the ears, too, because he knew how important this was from having helped with Calluna after hunting; and he lifted the thin, incredibly long forelegs to rub down the narrow little chest. Then, wrapping his coat carefully round the tiny creature, he lifted it into his arms. The foal took little notice, being weak beyond caring, and accepted all things as it found them. Its weight was quite considerable for an eleven-year-old to carry, small though it was; and through deep snow the task was doubly hard. But Paul trudged on, leaning back to balance the weight. The long legs dangled against his knees as he staggered down the hidden field-paths, and often he had to stop and sit down in the snow to get his breath and stretch his arms, the foal lying across his knees like a big, tired dog, and not moving anything except its small leaf-like ears.

So this was why Calluna swung fretting round her box; why she stared out over the snow across the door that was now padlocked as well as bolted. She knew - though no one else had guessed - that one of her foals lay out in Merlin Wood, desperately needing warmth and milk and dryness.

"I'm bringing it, Calluna. I'm bringing it, Calluna," Paul was saying over and over in his mind as he stumbled along, as if his thoughts might reach the mare and reassure her.

When at last he came to the farm and people rushed round him, and the foal was lifted from him, he could hardly straighten his stiff arms.

"Well, bless my soul!" Mr Boley kept saying, as they strode to the stable. "The old girl knew, all along."

"It looks pretty far gone, Dad," said Roy in the matter-of-fact tone that Paul could never understand.

"A bit weak," agreed his father, "and small wonder. But it's marvellous how they call pull round, sometimes."

"Listen! She's whinnying," said Paul, as they came into the yard. "She knows we've brought him!"

Calluna's lovely head was stretched over the door towards them as they came; and then she was licking the little foal all over its head and ears, and all over Paul's coat, too, wherever it came her way. Mr Boley laid the twin in the straw beside her, and Paul thought that he would never see anything in the whole of his life so moving as the mother's reunion with the lost one.

"Another little colt too," said Mr Boley. "Twin sons! Well, I'd sooner it'd been a single: twins don't often do so well. But, bless my soul, Paul, you're a hero if ever I've met one! My word, it's wonderful what they do know, isn't it?"

But all was not entirely as well as it seemed, for the second twin was very small and weak, and Calluna proved not to have enough milk to feed both of her foals. The bigger colt took well to mixed feeding, with cow's milk addition, but the small one drowsed in the straw and seemed only to hold on to his frail life by the lightness of a thread. For some days there was much anxiety about him, but no anxiety was greater than Paul's. All kinds of things were tried, such as boiling the milk to make it more digestible, and diluting it with water, and adding fresh yolk of egg, but nothing seemed to make any difference.

Mr Boley tried to comfort Paul with common sense and praise. "Well, look at it like this, son; if you've done nothing more than get Calluna to settle, that's enough for anyone to be proud of. I shouldn't set too much store on the little one living, if I were you. He doesn't seem to get on with cow's milk, and - well, even if he does pull through, I doubt if he'll ever be much good, you know."

"But, in a way, he's almost as if he were my colt," Paul said wistfully. "I mean, more especially mine than any other horse

31

ever was. If he died, I don't think I could ever be interested so much in anything, ever again."

"Tell you what," said Mr Boley, trying to cheer him up, "if he pulls through, you shall have him! There, what about that? Mind you, I doubt if he will - or that he'd be a credit to you when he grew up, either. More likely to grow up a weed, the way he's started. But there it is - yours, if you want him!"

Paul simply couldn't find a word to say, except, some minutes later, "Mine? Really? Oh I say! Thank you!"

After that, the only thing that mattered to him was the saving of his colt. He spent most of every day in the box with it, offering small bottles of warm milk mixture after the little that was available from Calluna. But the colt seemed somehow to grow frailer, more dreamy, more often with the long sweeping lashes lowered over his eyes; though by now his brother was bucking wickedly round the box and biting their mother's tail. In the mornings, Paul talked over these things with old Mr Terrell.

"Well now," said Tim thoughtfully one day, settling his postman's cap, "you might try a bit of goats' milk, p'raps. Wonderful, that is, for rearing delicate young things - animal or human, the both. Very digestible, is goat's milk, see." Paul stared at him, thinking away backwards. "Mr Terrell - that nanny goat you told me about -"

Old Tim nodded. "I reckon she's still available. But Will Fletcher, he don't reckon to sell no milk. Says it pays him better to feed it to his pigs. 'Sides, he's a good long way from Partridge Farm, son."

"I know, I don't want to buy the milk, but the goat," said Paul. "I want to have it at the farm, near the colt, so that he can have a little often; and really fresh."

Tim Terrell looked at him doubtfully for a moment, although it had really been his own idea in the first place. Then he said, "Well, it's your money, old son. And, after all, as I said before, a goat's a useful thing to have."

Paul went out to Will Fletcher's smallholding that same morning. The snow had all thawed away now, and blackbirds were singing in softly greening hedges. Will Fletcher fetched out the nanny goat to show Paul, and expressed himself willing to take thirty pounds for her, without guarantee (because he was a cautious man) except for his word that she was giving half a gallon a day and was quiet to milk and handle, her name being Milkmaid. She was a nice, intelligent-looking creature with a white coat as white as the snow the colt had been born in, and Paul led her away gratefully, at once, with the promise of sending out his money by Mr Terrell the next day.

He took the nanny goat straight to Partridge Farm, though it was nearly four miles from Will Fletcher's place, and she trotted along willingly enough on the end of her rope, though plainly much astonished at all this tramping. Mr Boley was quite agreeable to Paul's establishing her in a spare loose box near Calluna's; and, until he managed to teach himself to hand-milk, the cowman came along and milked a bottleful when needed, as well as supplying a pile of hay and roots and dairynuts which were things Paul had somehow not thought about, in the emergency.

It was even as Tim Terrell had said. Where all else failed, the goat's milk seemed to agree with the small one, and slowly he began to look less dreamy and shadowy taking a growing interest in the things around him. When, after a day or two, Paul brought his goat right into the loose box, and taught the colt to suckle properly, the real recovery began. Folding down loosely on his knees to reach the low udder, and wriggling his bushy little tail, the colt took to feeding from Milkmaid at once. As Mr Boley said, from that day you could almost see him growing. Within a week, he also was bucking round the loose box, and Mr Boley came and watched him one morning when Paul was leading Milkmaid out to her tether in the orchard.

"Bless my soul!" he said, laughing at the twin colts' antics. "I half regret saying I'd give him to you. Getting on fine, now, isn't he? You'd never credit it."

"Let me put Milkmaid out," begged Roy. "I know about moving her tether."

"All right," said Paul happily, handing over the head-rope. He was so happy, now, that he would have agreed to almost anything. Realising this, Roy suddenly said, "When the colt's weaned, I'll swap you my air-gun for Milkmaid. I think she's rather nice. And I could sell her kids too."

"I'll think about it," said Paul, leaning over the stable door to look at his colt - his very own colt.

"Time you named him, isn't it?" asked Mr Boley.

"I have," said Paul. "His name is Sure Magic."

"Sure what? Magic? Funny name, that. Why Magic?"

"Oh well - it just suits him, I think."

Mr Boley suddenly laughed. "Oh, I see! Of course - because he was born in Merlin Wood!"

"Well, partly," said Paul evasively. Then: "I don't suppose there really is any magic, do you, Mr Boley?" He sounded half doubtful, trying again to remember if he had wished before he saw those leaf-like ears in the snowdrift.

"Well - not quite magic, perhaps," said Mr Boley thoughtfully. Funny thing, though. Parson was talking about it, one Sunday in the snow-time. He was quoting someone, and he said, 'There are more things in heaven and earth than this world dreams of.' But I took it he was thinking of miracles."

"I know," said Paul slowly, remembering old Tim Terrell, and then he added, "Perhaps that's just what magic means."

ALICE THROUGH THE LOOKING GLASS
An Extract

Lewis Carroll

Alice has been meeting some of the characters from the chessboard. Now she meets the knights.

At this moment her thoughts were interrupted by a loud shouting of "Ahoy! Ahoy! Check!" and a Knight, dressed in crimson armour, came galloping down upon her, brandishing a great club. Just as he reached her, the horse stopped suddenly: "You're my prisoner!" the Knight cried, as he tumbled off his horse.

Startled as she was, Alice was more frightened for him than for herself at the moment, and watched him with some anxiety as he mounted again. As soon as he was comfortably in the saddle, he began once more "You're my - " but here another voice broke in "Ahoy! Ahoy! Check!" and Alice looked round in some surprise for the new enemy.

This time it was a White Knight. He drew up at Alice's side, and tumbled off his horse just as the Red Knight had done: then he got on again, and the two Knights sat and looked at each other without speaking. Alice looked from one to the other in some bewilderment.

"She's my prisoner, you know!" the Red Knight said at last.

"Yes, but then I came and rescued her!" the White Knight replied.

"Well, we must fight for her, then," said the Red Knight, as he took up his helmet (which hung from the saddle, and was something like the shape of a horse's head), and put it on.

"You will observe the Rules of Battle, of course?" the White Knight remarked, putting on his helmet too.

"I always do," said the Red Knight, and they began banging away at each other with such fury that Alice got behind a tree to be out of the way of the blows.

"I wonder, now, what the Rules of Battle are," she said to herself, as she watched the fight, timidly peeping out from her hiding-place: "One rule seems to be that, if one Knight hits the other, he knocks him off his horse, and if he misses, he tumbles off himself – and another Rule seems to be that they hold their clubs in their arms, as if they were Punch and Judy. What a noise they make when they tumble, just like fire-irons falling into the fender! And how quiet the horses are! They let them get on and off them just as if they were tables!"

Another Rule of Battle, that Alice had not noticed, seemed to be that they always fell on their heads, and the battle ended with their both falling off in this way, side by side: when they got up again, they shook hands, and then the Red Knight mounted and galloped off.

"It was a glorious victory, wasn't it?" said the White Knight, as he came up panting.

"I don't know," Alice said doubtfully. "I don't want to be anybody's prisoner. I want to be a Queen."

"So you will, when you've crossed the next brook," said the White Knight. "I'll see you safe to the end of the wood – and then I must go back, you know. That's the end of my move."

"Thank you very much," said Alice. "May I help you off with your helmet?" It was evidently more than he could manage by himself; however she managed to shake him out of it at last.

"Now one can breathe more easily," said the Knight, putting back his shaggy hair with both hands, and turning his gentle face and large mild eyes to Alice. She thought she had never seen such a strange-looking soldier in all her life.

"Now help me on. I hope you've got your hair well fastened on?" he continued, as they set off.

"Only in the usual way," Alice said, smiling. For a few minutes she walked on in silence, every now and then stopping to help the poor Knight, who certainly was not a good rider.

Whenever the horse stopped (which it did very often), he fell off in front; and whenever it went on again (which it generally did rather suddenly), he fell off behind. Otherwise he kept on pretty well, except that he had a habit of now and then falling off sideways; and as he generally did this on the side on which Alice was walking, she soon found that it was the best plan not to walk quite close to the horse.

"I'm afraid you've not had much practice in riding," she ventured to say, as she was helping him up from his fifth tumble.

The Knight looked very much surprised, and a little offended at the remark. "What makes you say that?" he asked, as he scrambled back into the saddle, keeping hold of Alice's hair with one hand, to save himself from falling over on the other side.

"Because people don't fall off quite so often, when they've had much practice."

"I've had plenty of practice," the Knight said very gravely: "plenty of practice!"

Alice could think of nothing better to say than "Indeed?" but she said it as heartily as she could. They went on a little way in silence after this, the Knight with his eyes shut, muttering to himself, and Alice watching anxiously for the next tumble.

"The great art of riding," the Knight suddenly began in a loud voice, waving his right arm as he spoke, "is to keep -" Here the sentence ended as suddenly as it had begun, as the Knight fell heavily on the top of his head exactly in the path where Alice was walking.

She was quite frightened this time, and said in an anxious tone, as she picked him up, "I hope no bones are broken?"

"None to speak of," the Knight said, as if he didn't mind breaking two or three of them. "The great art of riding, as I was saying, is - to keep your balance. Like this, you know -"

He let go of the bridle, and stretched out both his arms to show Alice what he meant, and this time he fell flat on his back, right under the horse's feet.

"Plenty of practice!" he went on repeating, all the time that Alice was getting him on his feet again. "Plenty of practice!"

"It's too ridiculous!" cried Alice, getting quite out of patience. "You ought to have a wooden horse on wheels, that you ought!"

"Does that kind go smoothly?" the Knight asked in a tone of great interest, clasping his arms round the horse's neck as he spoke, just in time to save himself from tumbling off again. "Much more smoothly than a live horse," Alice said, with a little scream of laughter, in spite of all she could do to prevent it.

"I'll get one," the Knight said thoughtfully to himself. "One or two – several."

KASHTANKA An Abridged Story
Chekhov

A young, copper-coloured dog, a combination of dachshund and mongrel with a nose like a fox's, was running up and down on the pavement, looking worried. Every now and again she paused, and lifting one frozen paw and then the other, whimpered, trying to understand how she had got lost.

She remembered very well what she had been doing during the day and how she had ended up on this unknown pavement.

The day had begun when her master, the carpenter Looka Alexandrych, put on his hat, picked up something wooden, wrapped it in a red handkerchief and said to her: "Come on Kashtanka."

She emerged from underneath the work-bench where she had been resting on wood shavings, had a good long stretch and ran after her master. Looka Alexandrych's customers lived a long way away, so that to reach all of them, the carpenter had to stop every so often at a tavern. Kashtanka remembered that during the journey she had behaved very badly. Happy to be taken for a walk, she leapt about, rushed barking at horse-trams, ran into back-yards and chased other dogs. The carpenter kept losing sight of her, and had to stop and shout at her angrily. Once he even caught her by her ear and pinched it, shook her and said very clearly: "you are a real pest!" After calling on his customers, Looka Alexandrych visited his sister and then a friend who was a book-binder; from there he went to a tavern and then to another friend and so on. So, when Kashtanka found herself on an unknown pavement, it was already evening and the carpenter was very drunk. He spoke to Kashtanka, calling to her and saying: "You are a lowly creature, a kind of insect. Compared to a man, you're like a carpenter compared to a cabinet-maker..."

Suddenly music blared out as he was talking to her. Kashtanka looked round and saw soldiers marching along the street towards her. As she hated music because it made her nervous she started howling and running about. The carpenter wasn't afraid at all, to her surprise, and he did not yelp but grinned and stood to attention, holding his hand to his hat in salute, with his fingers spread out. Seeing that her master was not annoyed with her, Kashtanka barked even louder and, driven mad by the noise, rushed across the road to the other side.

When she felt better, the music was no longer playing and the regiment of soldiers had gone. She ran across to the place where she had left her master, but he had disappeared. She rushed forward, then back, dashed across the road again but the carpenter seemed to have vanished into thin air. Kashtanka began sniffing the pavement, hoping to track her master by the smell of him, but someone must have already passed along, wearing new rubber boots, and all the smells had become mixed up with the smell of rubber so that she couldn't sort them out.

It was getting dark. The street lamps came on and lights appeared in the windows of houses. Snow started to fall in large flakes. Strange 'customers' passed Kashtanka in both directions without stopping, so that she couldn't see where she was going and she got caught up with their legs.

When it became totally dark, Kashtanka became very frightened. She stood right up against the porch of a house and began to whimper. She was tired out after her day with Looka Alexandrych, her ears and paws were like ice, and she was very hungry.

When the soft, fluffy snow had totally covered her back and she fell, exhausted, into a fitful sleep the door of the porch suddenly opened, and struck her on the side. She jumped up. A man came out through the door. He could not help but see her, as she yelped and got in the way of his feet. He bent down and said: "Where have you come from, doggy? Sorry, did I hurt you, poor little thing! Don't be angry, please."

Kashtanka looked at the stranger through the snowflakes and saw a short, fat little man with a puffy, clean-shaven face. He was wearing a top hat and a fur coat.

"What are you crying for?" he asked, brushing the snow off her back. "Where's your master? I suppose you are lost. What are we to do with you, poor thing?"

Hearing a nice, friendly voice, albeit a stranger's, Kashtanka licked his hands and whined some more. "Oh, you're a lovely, funny dog!" said the stranger. "Just like a fox. Come along with me then. Perhaps, you will be useful for something."

Only half an hour later she was sitting on the floor in a large room, her head on one side, giving this new stranger a questioning but affectionate look. He was having his dinner. He threw bits at her and since she was so hungry she bolted the food down, without noticing the taste. But the more she ate the hungrier she felt.

"Your master certainly didn't feed you very well," the stranger was saying, as he saw the amazing greed with which she gulped her food. "And how thin you are, just skin and bones."

Kashtanka ate a lot, but was still not satisfied. After supper she lay down in the middle of the room, stretched out her paws and feeling a pleasant drowsiness, began to wag her tail. While her new master, leaned back in his armchair, smoking a cigar, she asked herself which place was the nicest of the two - the carpenter's or the stranger's? The stranger's house was unattractive and badly decorated; besides the armchairs, sofa, the lamp and carpets he had nothing, and the room seemed very empty. The carpenter's flat, however, was full of things: he had a table, a work-bench, piles of shavings and many tools as well as a starling in a cage ... The stranger's place did not smell at all, whilst at the carpenter's there was always a smell of glue, varnish and shavings. The stranger, however, had one advantage - he gave her lots to eat, and while Kashtanka was sitting near the table gazing up at him affectionately, he had not hit her at all, or stamped his feet at her or shouted, "Get out you horrible animal!"

When her new master had finished his cigar, he went and fetched a small mattress. "Hey, dog, come here!" he said, putting the mattress down beside the sofa, "Lie down and have a sleep." Kashtanka stretched herself on the mattress and shut her eyes. She heard some barking in the street and wanted to answer it but suddenly sadness took hold of her. She remembered Looka Alexandrych and his small son Fedyushka, and her cosy little spot under the work bench. She remembered how, in the long, dark winter evenings, while the carpenter worked or read the paper aloud, Fedyushka used to play with her. He would pull her out from under the bench by her legs and make her do such tricks that she used to see stars and ache all over. He made her walk on her hind legs, pretended that she was a bell by pulling her tail so hard that she barked and howled, gave her tobacco to sniff. One of his tricks really caused her a lot of pain – Fedyushka would tie a piece of meat on the end of a piece of string and give it to Kashtanka; when she had swallowed it, he would pull it back from her stomach by the string, amidst peels of laughter. Kashtanka whimpered all the more as she remembered these events.

Soon, however, tiredness and warmth made her forget her sadness and she dozed off. When she woke up, it was already light and the street was noisy. There was no one in the room. Kashtanka stretched herself, and walked around the room. She sniffed around the corners and the furniture, but found nothing very interesting. There was another door, besides the door into the hall. She thought for a moment, scratched at it with both paws, opened it and walked into the next room. There on the bed, under a brown blanket, the stranger was asleep. She smelled the stranger's clothes and boots and decided that they smelled strongly of horse. There was another closed door which led out from the bedroom. Kashtanka pawed at the door, pushed it with her body, opened it and at once smelt a very strange smell. Imagining the worst, she growled and entered the little room with dirty wallpaper but was so scared she immediately backed out again. She could see something very odd. His neck and head close to the ground, his wings spread out, a grey goose was walking straight towards her, hissing. A little way away from him, on a small mattress, lay a white tom-cat. Seeing Kashtanka, he leapt up, arched his back, raised his tail, and with his fur standing up, hissed. The dog was now very afraid, but not wishing to show it, barked loudly and flew at the cat. The cat hissed and lashed out at Kashtanka with his paw. Kashtanka backed away, sat down on her haunches and, stretching out her nose towards the cat, started barking shrilly. Meanwhile, the goose came up to her from behind and gave her a painful peck on the back. Kashtanka leapt up and dashed at the goose ...

"Now, what's going on here?" They heard a loud, angry voice and in came the stranger. "What is the meaning of this? Back to your own places, at once!"

He approached the cat, tapped him on his arched back and said, "What are you up to, Fyodor Timofyeich? Beginning a fight, you old rascal! Lie down."

Then turning to the goose, he shouted: "Go to your place, Ivan Ivanych!"

The cat lay down on his little mattress and shut his eyes. He was cross with himself for having lost his temper. Kashtanka whined, offended and the goose stretched out his neck and started to chatter on and on in a great rush but one couldn't understand a word he said.

"All right, all right," the master said yawning. "You must all live in peace and friendship." He stroked Kashtanka and said, "As for you, don't be frightened. These are good pets, they won't hurt you. But what shall we call you?" He thought for a moment and then said: "We'll call you Auntie. Understand? Auntie." And having said the name a few times, he walked out. A month went by. Kashtanka had become used to being fed a delicious dinner every evening and being called 'Auntie'. She had also grown used to the stranger and to her new friends. Her life went very well. Every day began in the same way. Usually, Ivan Ivanych was the first to wake up. He would go over to 'Auntie' or the cat, curve his neck and start talking about something very enthusiastically but totally incomprehensibly as before. At first when he did this, Kashtanka thought that he talked so much because he was very bright, but after a time she lost her respect for him. Now, when he came up and started his long speeches, she no longer wagged her tail but took no notice of him and only growled.

Fyodor Timofyeich, on the other hand was a different type of gentleman. When he woke up, he was very quiet and kept his eyes shut. Obviously he didn't want to wake up very much because he didn't find life much fun. Nothing interested him; he was indifferent to most things and didn't even enjoy his food. The lessons the master gave the goose and the cat, and dinner-time made the days very interesting, but evenings were very dull. Usually, the master would drive off somewhere, taking the goose and cat with him. Left alone, Kashtanka would lie on her mattress and become very sad. She wouldn't feel like eating or barking or running about. During these times, two vague images appeared in her imagination; she felt affectionate towards them, but couldn't understand why. When she imagined them, she began to wag her tail and she seemed to know that some time, somewhere she had known and loved them ... And, as she fell asleep, she thought she could smell glue, wood shavings and varnish.

When she had grown used to her new life and had become a well-fed and well-cared for dog instead of a skinny, bony mongrel her master patted her one day and said: "It's time for you to learn some tricks, Auntie. Would you like to be a performer?"

And Kashtanka learnt all sorts of clever things. She was taught to stand and walk on her hind legs and jump up on her hind legs and snatch a lump of sugar held by the master high above her head. During the next few lessons she had to dance, run round in circles on a long lead, howl to music, ring the bell and fire the pistol, and by the end of the month she could take Fyodor Tomofyeich's place in the Egyptian pyramid very successfully and very happily. She learned fast and was pleased with herself. She ran in circles with her tongue out and jumped through hoops. But riding astride Fyodor Timofyeich gave her the greatest pleasure. As she performed each trick she barked and barked and her master, astonished and delighted with her, rubbed his hands together and kept saying, "What a talent! A real talent! You are a great success."

And Auntie grew used to the word 'talent' so that every time the master said it she jumped up and looked around as if it were her name.

Auntie was having a dog's dream: she was being chased by a road sweeper and she woke up frightened. She was not usually afraid of the dark but now she felt nervous and wanted to bark. Auntie closed her eyes, knowing that the quicker you got to sleep, the sooner the morning would come. But suddenly, quite close to her, she heard a strange noise, which made her jump and leap to her feet. The cry came from Ivan Ivanych, but it was not his usual chattering, persuasive voice but a wild, piercing and unnatural shriek. Unable to see anything in the dark and not understanding, Auntie felt even more scared and growled.

"Kghe-kghe," cried Ivan Ivanych. Awake again, Auntie sat up and started barking. It seemed that a stranger was shrieking. Then she heard the sound of slippered feet and the master, wearing a dressing gown and carrying a candle came in. The flickering light danced over the dirty wallpaper and the ceiling, and drove away the dark. Auntie saw that there was no stranger in the room but instead Ivan Ivanych was sitting on the floor. His wings were spread out, his beak open, and he looked tired and thirsty. Old Fyodor Timofyeich was not asleep either. Like the dog, he must have heard the shrieks.

"Ivan Ivanych, what's the matter?" the master asked the

goose. "Why are you screeching? Are you ill?"

The goose was silent. The master felt his neck, stroked him on the back and said, "You're an odd fellow. You won't sleep and then you stop others from sleeping."

Then the master went out and took away the light but Auntie was still afraid. The goose was quiet but the dog felt again as if there was somebody in the room. She thought that something bad was about to happen. Fyodor Timofyeich was also restless.

"Kghe, kghe," shouted Ivan Ivanych.

The master came back. The goose was sitting in the same pose. His eyes were closed.

"Ivan Ivanych!" called the master.

The goose did not stir. The master sat down on the floor, looked at him for a moment in silence, then said, "Ivan Ivanych! Whatever is the matter? Are you dying? Oh now I remember! It's because a horse trod on you today. Oh my God!"

Auntie did not understand what the master was saying but she could see by his face that he too was expecting something awful to happen. She moved her head towards the window, where she imagined a stranger was staring in and started to howl.

"He's dying, Auntie," said the master and threw his hands in the air. The master, who had turned very pale, returned to his bedroom, sighing and shaking his head. Auntie was afraid to stay in the dark, and followed him. He sat down on his bed and kept saying: "Good God, what are we going to do?"

Auntie sat close to his feet and not understanding why she felt so sad or why everyone was so upset, she watched his every movement. Fyodor Timofyeich, who hardly ever left his mattress, also came into the bedroom and rubbed himself against his master's feet. He shook his head as if trying to get rid of nasty thoughts and looked under the bed.

The master got a saucer and poured some water into it for the goose. "Drink Ivan Ivanych," he said gently.

But Ivan Ivanych did not move. "No, we can't do anything

more for him," the master sighed. "Ivan Ivanych is gone."

Tear drops crept down the master's cheeks. Auntie and Fyodor Timofyeich didn't understand what had happened and looked at the goose in terror.

"Poor Ivan Ivanych!" the master said sadly. "How shall I manage without you?"

Auntie imagined that the same thing was going to happen to her, that she too, might close her eyes, stretch out her paws and be looked at by everyone. Fyodor Timofyeich felt the same. He had never looked so gloomy and miserable before.

Dawn was breaking and soon the caretaker came, picked the goose up by its legs and took it away. Then the old woman came and took away the little trough.

One fine evening the master came into the room with the dirty wallpaper and, rubbing his hands together, said, "Well, today I'm going to take you, Auntie and Fyodor Timofeyich with me. You, Auntie, will replace the late Ivan Ivanych in the Egyptian pyramid. Devil alone knows what will happen. Nothing's been rehearsed enough. We'll disgrace ourselves, I expect."

He went out again and came back a minute later wearing his fur coat and hat. He picked up the cat and put him inside his fur coat. "Auntie come on," said the master.

Without understanding anything but wagging her tail, Auntie followed. A few minutes later, she was sitting in a sleigh at the master's feet, feeling him shiver with cold and listening to him muttering, "We'll disgrace ourselves ... we'll be sunk..."

The sleigh stopped in front of a large odd, round-shaped house. At the front there were three glass doors and bright shining lights. There were lots of people milling around and a number of horses trotting up to the doors but no dogs were to be seen.

The master picked up Auntie and threw her inside his fur coat where the cat was already nestling. It was dark and stuffy inside, but warm. Auntie gave Fyodor Timofyeich a lick on his ear, and wanting to make himself more comfortable, stuck her head out by mistake. She immediately drew it back in with a growl, for she thought she had seen an enormous room, full of monsters. From behind barriers many ugly faces were staring at her: noses of horses and animals with great horns or very long ears, and one huge fat muzzle which had a tail instead of a nose and two long bare bones sticking from its mouth.

The cat mewed but just then the master opened his coat and said "Hop!" and the two animals jumped to the floor. They were now in a small room with no furniture except a table and mirror, a stool and a light. Fyodor Timofyeich licked his coat which had been ruffled by Auntie, then went and lay down under the stool. The master began to dress up like a clown. Auntie was confused and was ready to run away from this multicoloured figure. The lights and the smells also filled her with fear and she was sure she was going to meet some horror such as the fat muzzle with a tail instead of a nose. Also, somewhere music began to play and a roar she did not understand could be heard from time to time. Fyodor Timofyeich's behaviour comforted her a little, since he took no notice of anything and lay dozing calmly under the stool. "Monsieur George, please!" someone shouted.

The master got up, pulled the cat from under the stool and put him in the suitcase. "Come here, Auntie," he said gently.

Auntie, not understanding, stood by him. He kissed her on the head and made her lie down beside the cat. Then darkness enclosed them completely. Auntie trod on the cat, scratched the inside of the case, but in her terror could not make a sound, while the suitcase swung about. "Here I am, here I am," shouted the master.

After that, Auntie felt the suitcase strike something hard, and stop swinging. A loud roar was heard. Someone was being slapped, probably the monster with a tail instead of a nose, and he was roaring so loudly that the locks of the suitcase shuddered. The master's laughter could be heard, "Ha" he shouted, doing his best to be heard above the roar. "Ladies and Gentlemen, I come straight from the station. My Gran's just passed away and left me her belongings. This suitcase is very heavy - I expect it's full of gold. Ha-a! Suppose it contains a million? In a moment we will open it and see!"

The suitcase lock clicked. Bright lights burst in on Auntie. She leapt out of the case and, deafened by the roar, began rushing round and round her master and barking furiously. "Ha!" shouted the master. "Dear Uncle Fyodor Timofyeich! My dear Auntie! My dear next-of-kin."

He threw himself down on the sand, snatched the cat and the dog and hugged them. Auntie looked around her - she couldn't move for a minute - she was so dazzled by this new world. Then she broke out of her master's arms and spun round and round like a spinning top. Bright lights shone down on her and wherever she looked there were faces from the ground right up to the ceiling.

"Auntie, please sit down," shouted the master.

Remembering what that meant, "Auntie leapt on to a chair and sat, looking at her master. His face was set in a wide, immoveable smile and he was laughing, jumping up and down, and trying to look as though he was having a great time. Auntie thought that he must be truly happy, and lifting her foxy muzzle, she barked with delight.

"You sit for a bit, Auntie," the master said. "Dear Uncle and myself are going to dance the Kamarinsky." Fyodor Timofyeich danced in a bored, gloomy way and it was obvious from his movements that he hated the crowd, the lights, the master and himself. When he had finished, he yawned and sat down.

"Well, Auntie," said the master, "we'll begin by singing and dance afterwards. All right?"

He took a small pipe from his pocket and began playing. Auntie, who hated music, moved restlessly on her chair and howled. Roaring and clapping broke out on all sides. The master bowed, and kept playing. When he reached one very high note, a loud "Ah!" rang out from the gallery. "Look Dad!" shouted a child's voice. "That's Kashtanka!"

"So it is!" agreed a rather drunk, high pitched voice. "Kashtanka! Good Lord, Fedyushka! It is Kashtanka. Kashtanka!" Someone in the gallery whistled and two voices, one of a child, the other of a man, called loudly: "Kashtanka, Kashtanka!"

Auntie, startled, looked up to where the noise was coming from. She could see two faces, one hairy and drunken, the other puffy and red-cheeked. The memory returned and she fell off her chair, wriggled about in the sand, then jumped up and yelping joyfully, dashed towards those faces. A roar broke out again and she could hear the child's voice, "Kashtanka, Kashtanka."

Auntie leapt over the barrier, over someone's shoulder and found herself in a box. To get to the next level, she had to leap over a high wall. Auntie jumped but didn't reach the top and slid down again. After that she was passed from person to person, licking hands and faces, and moving higher and higher until she reached the gallery.

Half an hour later Kashtanka was walking along the street behind the people who smelled of glue and varnish. Looka Alexandrych was swaying from side to side and was muttering, "As for you Kashtanka, you're neither one thing or the other ... Compared to a man you're like a carpenter compared to a cabinet-maker."

Beside him marched Fedyushka, wearing his father's hat. Kashtanka looked at their backs and it seemed to her that she had been walking behind them for a long time, and that her usual life had not been interrupted even for a minute.

She remembered the small room with the grubby wallpaper, the goose, Fyodor Timofyeich, delicious suppers, the lessons, the circus, but all this now seemed to her to be a long, confused and unhappy dream.

BLACK BEAUTY An Extract
Anna Sewell

Black Beauty tells of his journey to fetch the Doctor.

One night I had eaten my hay and was laid down in my straw fast asleep, when I was suddenly awoken by the stable bell ringing very loud. I heard the door of John's house open, and his feet running up to the Hall. He was back again in no time; he unlocked the stable door, and came in, calling out, "Wake up, Beauty, you must go well now, if ever you did," and almost before I could think, he had got the saddle on my back and the bridle on my head; he just ran round for his coat, and then took me at a quick trot up to the Hall door. The Squire stood there with a lamp in his hand.

"Now John," he said, "ride for your life, that is for your mistress's life; there is not a moment to lose; give this note to Doctor White; give your horse a rest at the Inn and be back as soon as you can."

John said, "Yes sir," and was on my back in a minute. The gardener who lived at the lodge had heard the bell ring, and was ready with the gate open, and away we went through the Park and through the village and down the hill till we came to the toll-gate. John called very loud and thumped upon the door: the man was soon out and flung open the gate.

"Now," said John, "do you keep the gate open for the Doctor; here's the money," and off he went again.

There was before us a long piece of level road by the river side; John said to me, "Now Beauty, do your best," and so I did; I wanted no whip nor spur, and for two miles I galloped as fast as I could lay my feet to the ground; I don't believe that my old grandfather who won the race at Newmarket could have gone faster. When we came to the bridge, John pulled me up a little and patted my neck. "Well done, Beauty! Good old fellow," he said. He would have let me go slower, but my spirit was up, and I was off again as fast as before. The air was frosty, the moon was bright, it was very pleasant; we came through a village, then through a dark wood, then uphill, then downhill, till after an eight mile run we came to the town, through the streets and into the Market Place. It was all quite still except for the clatter of my feet on the stones – everybody was asleep. The church clock struck three as we drew up at Doctor White's door. John rang the bell twice, and then knocked at the door like thunder. A window was thrown up, and Doctor White put his head out and said, "What do you want?"

"Mrs Gordon is very ill, sir; master wants you to go at once, he thinks she will die if you cannot get there – here is a note."

"Wait," he said, "I will come."

He shut the window, and was soon at the door.

"The worst of it is," he said, "that my horse has been out all day and is quite done up; my son has just been sent for, and he has taken the other. What is to be done? Can I have your horse?"

"He has come at a gallop nearly all the way, sir, and I was to give him a rest here; but I think my master would not be against it if you think fit, sir."

"All right", he said, "I will soon be ready."

John stood by me and stroked my neck, I was very hot. The Doctor came out with his riding whip.

"You need not take that, sir," said John. "Black Beauty will go till he drops; take care of him sir, if you can, I should not like any harm to come to him."

"No! No! John," said the Doctor, "I hope not," and in a minute we had left John far behind.

I will not tell about our way back; the Doctor was a heavier man than John, and not so good a rider; however, I did my very best. The man at the toll-gate had it open. When we came to the hill, the Doctor drew me up. "Now, my good fellow," he said, "take some breath." I was glad he did, for I was nearly spent, but that breathing helped me on, and soon we were in the Park. Joe was at the lodge gate, my master was at the Hall door, for he had heard us coming. He spoke not a word; the

Doctor went into the house with him, and Joe led me to the stable. I was glad to get home, my legs shook under me, and I could only stand and pant. I had not a dry hair on my body, the water ran down my legs, and I steamed all over – Joe used to say, like a pot on the fire. Poor Joe! He was young and small, and as yet he knew very little, and his father, who would have helped him, had been sent to the next village; but I am sure he did the very best he knew. He rubbed my legs and my chest, but he did not put my warm cloth on me; he thought I was so hot I should not like it. Then he gave me a bucket full of water to drink; it was cold and very good, and I drank it all; then he gave me some hay and some corn, and thinking he had done right, he went away. Soon I began to shake and tremble, and turned deadly cold, my legs ached, my loins ached, and my chest ached, and I felt sore all over. Oh! how I wished for my warm thick cloth as I stood and trembled. I wished for John, but he had eight miles to walk, so I lay down in my straw and tried to go to sleep. After a long while I heard John at the door; I gave a low moan, for I was in great pain. He was at my side in a moment stooping down by me; I could not tell him how I felt; but he seemed to know it all; he covered me up with two or three warm cloths, and then ran to the house for some hot water; he made me some warm gruel which I drank, and then I think I went to sleep.

John seemed to be very much put out. I heard him say to himself, over and over again, "stupid boy! stupid boy! no cloth put on, and I dare say the water was cold too; boys are no good," but Joe was a good boy after all.

I was now very ill; a strong inflammation had attacked my lungs, and I could not draw my breath without pain. John nursed me night and day, he would get up two or three times in the night to come to me; my master, too, often came to see me.

"My poor Beauty," he said one day, "my good horse, you saved your mistress's life, Beauty! yes, you saved her life." I was very glad to hear that for it seems the Doctor had said if we had

53

been a little longer it would have been too late. John told my master he never saw a horse go so fast in his life, it seemed as if the horse knew what was the matter. Of course I did, though John thought not; at least I knew as much as this, that John and I must go at the top of our speed, and that it was for the sake of the mistress.

THE STORY OF FIDO

Miss A M Alleyne

Fido's master had to go a long journey across the country to a certain town, and he was carrying with him a large bag of gold to deposit at the bank there. This bag he carried on his saddle, for he was riding as in those days there were no trains, and he had to travel as quickly as he could.

Fido scampered cheerfully along at the horse's heels, and every now and then the man would call out to him, and Fido would wag her tail and bark back an answer.

The sun was hot and the road dusty, and poor Fido's little legs grew more and more tired. At last they came to a cool, shady wood, and the master stopped, dismounted, and tied his horse to a tree, and took his heavy saddle-bags from the saddle.

He laid them down very carefully and, pointing to them, said to Fido, "Watch them."

Then he drew his cloak about him, lay down with his head on the bags, and soon was fast asleep.

Little Fido curled herself up close to her master's head, with her nose over one end of the bags, and went to sleep too. But she did not sleep very soundly, for her master had told her to watch, and every few moments she would open her eyes and prick up her ears, in case anyone was coming.

Her master was tired and slept soundly and long - much longer than he had intended. At last he was awakened by Fido's licking his face. The dog saw that the sun was nearly setting, and knew that it was time for her master to go on his journey.

The man patted Fido and then jumped up, much troubled to find he had slept so long. He snatched up his cloak, threw it over his horse, untied the bridle, sprang into the saddle, and calling Fido, started off in great haste. But Fido did not seem ready to follow him. She ran after the horse and bit at his heels and then ran back again to the woods, and all the time barking furiously. This she did several times, but her master had no time to heed her and galloped away, thinking she would follow him.

At last the little dog sat down by the roadside, and looked

sorrowfully after her master, until he had turned a bend in the road. When he was no longer in sight she sprang up with a wild bark, and ran after him again. She overtook him just as he had stopped to water his horse at a brook that flowed across the road. She stood beside the brook and barked so savagely that her master rode back and called her to him; but instead of coming she darted off down the road still barking.

Her master did not know what to think, and began to fear that his dog was going mad. Mad dogs are afraid of water, and act in a strange way when they see it. While the man was thinking of this, Fido came running back again, and dashed at him furiously. She leapt at the legs of his horse, and even jumped up and bit the toe of her master's boot. Then she ran down the road again, barking with all her might.

Her master was now sure that she was mad, and taking out his pistol he shot at her. He rode away quickly, for he loved her dearly and could not bear to see her die.

He had not ridden very far when he stopped suddenly. He felt under his cloak for his saddle-bags. They were not there!

Could he have dropped them, or had he left them behind in the wood where he had rested?

He felt they must be in the wood, for he could not remember having picked them up or fastening them to his saddle. He turned his horse and rode back again as hard as he could.

When he came to the brook he sighed and said, "Poor Fido!" but though he looked about he could see nothing of her. When he crossed the brook he saw some drops of blood on the ground, and all along the road he still saw drops of blood. Tears came into his eyes, and he felt very sad and guilty, for now he understood why little Fido had acted so strangely. She knew that her master had left behind his precious bags of gold, and so she had tried to tell him in the only way she could.

All the way to the wood lay the drops of blood. At last he reached the wood, and there, all safe, lay the bags of gold, and beside them, with her little nose lying over one end of them, lay faithful Fido, who, you will be pleased to hear, recovered from her wound, and lived to a great age.

THE SLUGHEART

Lucy Bickersteth

Dr Craven turned round from the fire and greeted his wife with a teasing smile. "It's as bad as a new pup," he mocked. "Will it have to sleep in our room, my dear?"

"Arthur!"

He laughed outright at her indignation. "Well, they generally cry all the first night. Tell me honestly, was it crying when you went up just now?"

Mrs Craven nodded. "Poor little thing," she said; and crossing over to the fire she leaned against the mantelpiece. After a minute's silence she went on, "Arthur, I really am sorry for her. Think of it: separated from her mother for the first time and only just eleven!"

"Well," rejoined the doctor, "lots of little girls go to school younger than that, and school is a more terrifying experience than spending a few months with a harmless doctor and his wife, isn't it?"

"In a way. But – well, I suppose Betsy has been rather spoiled. She confided to me just now that as a rule her nanny sang to her till she went to sleep."

The doctor laughed.

"That's when I left her: I really couldn't undertake singing her to sleep; and now she's crying bitterly."

"Do her good," muttered the doctor. But he sighed and looked longingly at the door.

As he picked up the Spectator and smoothed its crumpled pages Dr Craven sighed again.

When Betsy woke next morning she got straight out of bed and leaned out of the window. "Good," she said to herself, and looked approvingly at the hazy blue sky, and the dew-drenched lawn. "I'm glad it's fine." She dressed, and waited impatiently for breakfast time.

Punctually at half-past eight she opened her door and ran softly downstairs. Mrs Craven was already in the dining room.

"Good morning, dear," she said, and kissed her. "I am so glad it's fine for your first morning."

"Yes. So shall I be able to go and have tea with those children you were telling me about?" Betsy said. And then she added shyly, "You will have time to take me, won't you?"

"Bless the child, of course I will! I'll take you over to the Hall and leave you there while I go on to the Women's Institute."

"What time must I be ready, please?"

"Three o'clock will be time enough," said Mrs Craven, and sat down to breakfast.

Betsy was the last to arrive at Beth Tresize's birthday party. With a quick-beating heart she made her way across the field. To her it seemed a silly medley of scuttling ponies and children. Nothing was still, except - yes, there was one still thing - an ugly roan hitched in the shade of a holly tree. No one noticed her, so she stole round quietly and stood beside the cob. Flies swarmed thickly round his dark eyes and tickled his velvety nose, but he did not seem to care. He dozed, breathing deep and sighing every now and then. Betsy knew nothing about horses; she had never stroked one in all her life till now, with a nervous, stiff hand, she patted the cob's nose.

He woke with a start, and stared resentfully at her. "Another child," he snorted. "They're all alike, nasty little things!" And he rested the other back leg and reached for a twig of hazel above his head. Unfortunately he had eaten all within his reach so, after searching round with lips well thrust out, he gave it up.

Betsy, though ignorant, was quick-witted. She understood his difficulty, and darting off, picked a good switch of hazel and ran back with it. Back went the cob's ears and he started away from her. Children with sticks annoyed him; and this one seemed worse than most; she meant to hit his head, so he snapped cunningly and caught the hazel. At once Betsy let go and fetched him another. Busily she ran to and fro, busily the cob's jaws worked, and the two were very happy. "Hullo!"

At the cheerful greeting Betsy turned round. "Hullo!" she echoed shyly.

The big pleasant-faced girl cocked a leg over her horse's neck and slipped to the ground. She advanced and shook hands with Betsy. "I'm Beth Tresize," she explained. "I suppose you're Betsy?"

Betsy nodded.

"And all these," went on the girl, "are my brothers, cousins, and friends. Billy!" she suddenly screamed, "Billy, don't ride Sam. He'll lame himself without a shoe. Billy, come here, you can ride the Slugheart."

A burst of laughter greeted her words.

"Come on!" shrilled a very small girl, obviously riding her mother's hunter. "Come on and watch Billy ride the Slugheart. What's the odds? Slug's favourite," she yelled. "I back the Slug." And she dashed up to join Beth by the holly tree, followed by Billy and the rest of the children.

Billy tied his white-faced Sam to the hazel tree in the bank and strode up to the Slugheart. The cob hung his head and flicked his short tail apprehensively. Quietly enough Billy unhitched the reins, tweaked them over the pony's head and swung up on to his back. He shortened up his reins. The cob did not move. He dug in his heels. Nothing happened.

"Look here, Beth," he demanded, "is this animal alive? Can it feel?" He kicked furiously into the cob's round sides and heaved at his mouth. The more he kicked and tugged the more the children laughed. They sat round on their ponies in a derisive ring mocking, advising, commiserating, till the boy's face flushed red with anger.

"Get behind the brute, someone, and give him one," he ordered: and the very small girl edged the hunter up alongside the bank and cracked her thong across Slugheart's hind-quarters. He raised a leg and kicked out, but he did not move. Crack! The whip curled about him and thud! His leg shot out and caught the bank. Again and again the whip cut him, and every time he kicked the bank. After a minute Beth pushed forward. "Drop it!" she ordered. "It's no use beating him. He's

60

past mending. My father gave him to me last summer to do what I liked with because he's spoilt. The breaker's boys misunderstood him, Daddy says; and he, being a stubborn colt, grew stubborner and stubborner till now he beats the worst mule in the King's army. See?"

Billy jumped off and hitched the unperturbed pony up to the holly tree again. "Well", he sighed, "if I can't ride Sam, and I can't ride Slug, I must walk, that's all." Then with sudden interest: "Beth, why do you keep that fool horse?"

"Because he's only an eight year old and it seems a shame to shoot him. But look here," Beth's blue eyes shone with mischief, "if anyone at any time can canter that cob in a figure of eight and take him over a jump three times running, I give him the pony for his own."

A yell of laughter greeted this speech.

"Safe offer!" scoffed the boy, Billy. "I'd sooner ride the Derby winner at a state funeral."

"You'd give him away?" Incredulous, Betsy asked the question.

Beth looked round and met Betsy's bewildered, dark eyes. The child was leaning forward, her hands clasped tightly together, her whole being tense with excitement.

Beth liked her; she nodded her head. "Of course I will," she said. "Would you like to try her now?"

But Betsy drew back. "No," she sighed. "Not now. I can't ride. I - I-I've never tried."

"Never ridden!" The children looked at one another in amazement; then altogether they offered "Here, try my pony!" "No, Tinkerbell's the quietest."

"Silly ass, he's a brute. Get up on my Dumpling; she'll teach you to ride."

Beth took command. "No," she said, "Betsy can ride Vagabond. She'll be the tenth person he's taught. Where is he?"

Little Molly Manners rode forward. "Here he is," she called, and slid from his back.

Vagabond pushed his aristocratic old face under Beth's arm, and she kissed him on the end of his nose. Next minute Betsy was in the saddle and an unreasoning terror possessed her. She clutched the reins, she leaned forward, her legs drew back and her heels kicked into his sides, and old Vagabond answered politely. With a gentle lurch he sprang to a canter; then he pulled up and stood still: he had left his rider behind.

"Bad luck!" Ill-concealed amusement lurked in Beth's voice. "Hop up again and I'll lead him."

But Betsy turned her back; tears trickled down her cheeks, fear and shame were in her heart and she could not speak. Billy began to whistle; all the children were extraordinarily embarrassed. Someone was crying, and just because she fell off too! Really it was rather the outside edge.

Then Beth, the eldest, found her wits. She ran after the sobbing child and said kindly: "You'd better go in and have tea with the grown-ups."

Betsy shook her head.

"Well, cut along home then, and" – with a mischievous twinkle, she added – "you may ride Slugheart any day next term you like, and term begins tomorrow."

Betsy's voice came through the strangling tears. "Thank you. Goodbye."

Next minute long-legged Beth was haring back to her friends; and lonely, disgraced little Betsy dragged her feet along the lane back to the doctor's house.

That evening Betsy discovered Geoffrey Brooke's famous horse book in the library and she carried it up to her bedroom and hid it in the drawer, under her best dress. For three days she studied that book in every spare moment she had; and that meant many hours, because the doctor and his wife were busy people and Betsy was left much to herself.

On the fourth day she set out for the field. In the doctor's garage she had unearthed a bridle and saddle and these she lugged with her. At the field gate she paused and stared in: there stood the Slugheart under the holly bush, just as if he were tied. Betsy's lips moved; she was remembering the book. "Quiet in all my movements," she whispered, "confident and fearless."

She opened the gate with exaggerated stealth and made her way slowly towards the cob, a happy smile on her face. The smile was to show confidence and fearlessness.

Slugheart looked at her and laid back his ears, but he did not run away. He sighed. With clumsy movements she threw the reins round his neck and held up the bridle. Slugheart shut his mouth firmly and gazed at the sky. The child could not reach his head. This was embarrassing. The book failed to give advice in the predicament of a horse's sky-gazing. Betsy was nonplussed. She tried coaxing.

"Oh Slugheart," she entreated, "please look down a minute. Give me your head for a minute. Oh please!"

If anything, Slugheart raised his head.

Somehow that reminded Betsy of hazel twigs. She left the bridle dangling round his neck and tiptoed to the hazel tree. Then, with her arms full of nice leafy twigs, she crept back.

"There!" she said, and dumped them on the grass under his nose.

As if by magic the Slug's head dropped, and with a tiny knicker of appreciation, he filled his mouth to overflowing. Now was her chance. She seized the bridle and held it in front of the horse's nose and he who had no real objection to a bridle, felt for the bit and sucked it in along with the hazels, and allowed her fumbling fingers to tweak his ears through the headpiece and fasten the throat lash.

Betsy stood back and surveyed him, her eyes shining with pride. She had bridled the horse alone; it seemed but a step to winning him for her very own. And, from this day onward, Slugheart was conscientiously put through a course of breaking as laid down in Colonel Brooke's inimitable book. Possibly he would not have recognised his methods but they were amazingly effective.

The happy days wore on. Hay harvest was over, and the corn fields gleamed like lost sunshine in the valleys. The term ended.

On the first morning of the summer holidays Betsy lay under a laurel tree in the shrubbery and cried. A tear dropped right on an ant as he hurried along; with renewed haste, he, as it were, shook himself, and passed on, intent on the business in hand. Several more ants appeared and Betsy tried to drop another tear on another ant. Then perversely, the tears stopped dropping and she sat up. Forlornly she thought, the Hall children have come home and for me the Slugheart is no more.

"Oh," she whimpered, "that girl, Beth, said, 'for the term'. If only she had said 'for always.' If only –"

Suddenly she grew rigid. Her lips parted and the red colour glowed under the brown of her cheeks.

"A figure of eight and over a jump. I will give him the pony for his own."

Betsy sprang to her feet. "But I can! I can!" she said aloud. "I can!" and she ran into the house.

Mrs Craven stood in the hall, an open letter in her hand. "Read this, Betsy," she said.

Betsy read:

"Dear Mrs Craven,
The children are having a gymkhana in Shoal Meadow this afternoon, and if your little friend cares to join them we should be delighted –"

Betsy read no farther. She lifted such a happy face to hers, that Mrs Craven wondered.

"Oh ," she stammered, "oh, oh but I'd love to go!" and she sped upstairs to her bedroom.

The first item on the afternoon's programme was tea, because as Beth explained, "the flies are so awful in the heat of the day; they drive the ponies crazy."

Betsy waited on the grass between Billy and Molly and had a good view of the ponies' hind-quarters. Eight of them there were, tied up in the shade of the south bank. Four neat-legged Dartmoors, Molly's mother's hunter Vagabond, the old thoroughbred Sam, Billy's pride and the winner of many gymkhana events, and at the end of the line, Slugheart. He was taking no interest in the other horses. At the moment his attention was concentrated on the task of ridding himself of a grey fly settled behind his ear. He shook his head. He blew his nose. He lashed his stumpy tail. All to no purpose. Then he had an idea. Carefully balancing on three legs, he raised a back one and brought it up to his head and the next minute the grey fly was squashed dead.

"Well done, ugly!" called Beth, who had seen the performance. "That freak has got a brain, if only he would use it."

Billy shook his head. "No Beth. He isn't even half-witted; he's –"

Molly interrupted him. "Yes Slug's a fool," she agreed. Then, turning to Beth: "I say, what events are you having after tea?"

Beth produced a sheet of paper and read aloud: "A prize of chocolate will be given to the rider of the handiest horse. To be voted by all present. There! Mother gave me that at lunch time; and all the visitors are coming at five o'clock."

A gasp of dismay greeted this speech. Then all the children fell to talking.

"Sam's a good pony, but too hot," explained Billy.

"Oh he's not," chorused the children.

"Now Ladybird –"

"No Molly. Ladybird's perfect. My little beast –"

Beth interrupted: "Vagabond's too big; he can't turn as quickly as your heath croppers. If only Slug were not impossible I'd ride him."

Betsy took her courage in both hands. "Please," the children stopped chattering to listen because of the quietness of her voice, "please, may I try the Slug, just for a joke?" she pleaded.

Beth shook her head. She was a kind girl and really hated other people to be discomfited.

"You may try Vagabond, and I'll whack the Slug round the course," she said.

It seemed to Betsy that they would hear her heart beat; but there was a stubborn gleam in her dark eyes as she repeated: "May I try Slugheart please? Not Vagabond."

Beth shrugged her shoulders. "Oh right you are," she said carelessly. "You can do what you like with the fool."

"Thank you."

Betsy was not unconscious of the pity and contempt that the others tried to hide. They remembered her tears and her failure last holidays, and until she could wipe out the memory by some act of outstanding prowess, they would not forget.

"They're coming!" Billy leapt to his feet with the words and ran to Sam.

Betsy looked and saw the little crowd of visitors crossing the field towards them and she too jumped up and went to Slugheart. He showed no sign of recognition. When the child, sweet-faced with love, looked at him, he yawned: only after she had pulled up the girths and slipped on the bridle, he dropped his head into the crook of her arm and breathed deep.

The grown-ups made themselves comfortable and waited for the children to begin.

At last they were ready, and Beth, on old Vagabond, rode across to the audience. Clearly and capably she explained: "There are eight entries. We all vote for the best: you and us. The pony judged to be the cleverest - handiest, you know - over the jumps and cantered in a figure of eight, wins. See?" Without waiting for an answer she wheeled and cantered back to the competitors.

"I'll go first because I know the course exactly, and you can watch and learn. Come on Vaga!"

Vagabond trotted to the start. For fifty yards they cantered straight ahead, then Beth bent him in and out of a figure of eight. It was a good attempt and the old horse answered well, but he was still and failed twice to change legs on the turn. Then they cantered on and popped over the first jump; on again and over the second. Last came an in-and-out; an upright and but room for a horse to change feet and another upright. Vagabond jumped in and stopped. He looked at the jump in front and decided not. But Beth was firm, she kept him straight to it, and suddenly he shot up and bucked over as ungainly as a mule. Beth came round his neck but righted herself and cantered steadily back to the children.

She allowed no waste of time in discussing things. "Next!" she ordered, and Molly pushed Ladybird forward. She did excellently till she got to the in-and-out and then she refused. She would not even jump in. In vain Molly urged and coaxed and kicked; the mare was determined. Then came a shrill call from Beth: "Disqualified!" And Molly wrenched Ladybird round, stuck in her heels, and galloped furiously back again.

Then, one by one, the Dartmoor ponies tried. Three did fairly well, but one little fellow would do nothing but whinny. When asked to canter he threw back his head and called loudly to his friends, and at the last jump he too was disqualified.

Sam and the Slugheart were left.

"Next!" said Beth.

Betsy had just realised her stirrups were much too long and was struggling to shorten them. "Billy please go; I'm not ready," she gasped, and Billy set off at a gallop.

Certainly Sam was a neat pony. He bent to the figure of eight like a polo pony, cleared the jumps like a trained show jumper, and nipped in and out with never a falter.

"Jolly good, Bill!" said Beth, and then she turned to Betsy. "You really want to try?" she questioned. And Betsy nodded.

Betsy mounted the Slug and shortened up her reins. Slug shook his red head and moved off kindly. Beth stared. Billy muttered, "He didn't jib. Oh!"

The roan horse wheeled round the starting flag and came at a brisk canter down the course. Then Betsy laid the reins across his neck and he turned; she reversed them, and the Slug, with ears tight back and dark eyes agleam, changed feet and swung left. It was a perfect figure of eight and the horse had neither slackened nor quickened.

"A little faster, Sluggie, a little faster," Betsy whispered, and leaned forward.

He took the first jump at a gallop.

"Now slow," the child entreated. She took a pull and then as good as dropped the reins. The horse slowed to a canter. He cocked an ear at the jump and cleared it, slow-soaring like a raven rising from a furrow. And as he landed his rein broke near the bit.

"Oh!" There was real disappointment in the sigh that broke from the onlookers, but Betsy took no notice.

"Right turn, Slug," she said and leaned to the right. He felt the pressure and turned. Still cantering he came to the in-and-out. He understood this very well and liked the game. Quickly he hopped over and in, changing feet and jumped out. It amused him so much that he broke in to a gallop and raced a few yards towards the visitors; but two hands on his neck were soothing and his friend was saying, "Steady!" So he did steady and answered the pressure on his neck and sides demurely and as sanely as if no broken rein flapped and dangled to his knees.

"Whoa!" Betsy brought him to a stand-still and slipped off his back. Then she realised that the visitors were hurrying across the field; the children were crowding round, and Beth, in front of the rest, was simply laughing with excitement.

"You - You - You!"

"Congratulations!" shouted Billy from the background. "You beat us fair and square. But Sam was second, wasn't he, Beth?"

But she did not hear him. "You -you-" she went on stammering, and suddenly got the words out with a rush.

"You're magic! and Slugheart is yours, and I'm glad."

For the second time, Betsy cried. She buried her face in the Slug's hot neck and sobbed.

Then she raised her face, flushed and starry-eyed. Close beside her stood two people who smiled happily, and one was holding out her arms.

"Mummy!" Then "Daddy!" she cried, "I've got a horse. Daddy, the Slugheart is actually mine."

And while Betsy clung round her mother's neck, dear old Slugheart ambled off to the hazel bush and ate methodically.

THE BLOTTING-PAPER DOG

E.S.

When the postcard came to say that he would arrive by the 5.30 train, Lorna was very much excited. But she wished she knew what kind of dog a Dalmatian was.

"Do you know, Jock?" she asked the cousin who lived next door.

"Just an ordinary dog, nice to stroke, who fights and hunts things," said he.

"Big or little?"

"Oh that depends."

"Rough or smooth?"

"Just middling."

"I wish he were a peke or a foxy," said Lorna. "I'd like a funny little nice dog."

When the hamper was brought up from the station, Lorna opened it. And there, blinking and wagging his tail, was the oddest dog she had ever seen. He was big for a pup, and his coat was white spotted with black, and his eyes were black with white lashes, and his tail was quite white. He looked like an animal out of Noah's Ark, but when you lifted him you found that he was soft as plush. When he was taken out of his basket and put on the rug his legs wobbled and he rolled right over.

"He's dreadfully cramped, poor darling," said Lorna's mother. "He's a big puppy, and he ought to have had more room."

"Will he grow up a very big dog?" asked Lorna.

"He'll be a fair size. And he'll want lots of exercise. These are the dogs that used to run by carriages when people drove horses."

"Oh - is he an old-fashioned kind of dog?" said Lorna.

"He's just like a bit of blotting-paper, isn't he?" said Jock. "A bit out of one of Lorna's exercise books, all smothered with blots."

"I must say he's the blottiest Dalmatian I've ever seen," said Lorna's father. "And I should think he's the hungriest, poor chap."

BP as Jock named him, short for Blotting Paper, was really a darling pup, and Lorna rather liked him, though she did wish he had not been quite so peculiar to look at. She hated it when the children in the street jeered at him and called him a plum pudding. She wished he would bite them, or at least, bark fiercely, but he didn't seem to care if people were nasty to him, and he jumped about and enjoyed himself as if everyone admired him.

"He's not a bad pup, but I wouldn't have chosen him for a birthday present," said Jock. "You'd have been far better with a really good fountain pen. That's what Aunt Lucy is going to give me. I'm to get it next Saturday afternoon. I'll put a few more blots on old BP for you then, if you like. He'd look smarter with one or two on that white tail. It comes so suddenly – it doesn't look as if it belongs to him."

"BP isn't coming to Aunt Lucy's," said Lorna. "She won't have pups in the house."

And when you went inside Aunt Lucy's house you understood why. All the rugs and carpets were of pale colours, which would have showed up every print of muddy paws, and all the chairs and tables had polished spindly legs, which would have been ruined by the marks of a pup's teeth.

There was a surprise waiting for Lorna.

"It isn't nearly such a good one as Jock's, of course," said Aunt Lucy, as she gave her a stumpy fountain pen. "But it writes quite nicely, they say, and it'll do to go on with till Christmas, or your next birthday."

"I should think so," said Lorna, much pleased. "Thank you very much, Aunt Lucy. May I put ink in it now?"

"No – wait till you get home, dear. And put down a newspaper then before you fill it."

Lorna tried the nib without ink in it, but she could not tell how it would write, and she felt rather out of it as Jock, whose pen was filled, covered an old sheet of wrapping-paper with his name and hers and pictures of idols and owls and cottages and skeletons. "Let me try yours, Jockie," she begged.

Jock looked rather doubtful. He was too fond of his new pen to want to give it up, even for a little time.

"You might let it leak," he said.

"I won't. Yours is the kind that won't leak, whatever happens. You can hold it upside down, you said. You can't hold mine upside down - that's why Aunt Lucy didn't want me to fill it."

"I tell you what," said Jock. "I'll see if I can squirt some of the ink out of mine and put it in yours. I don't think that would matter. We'll try it over the fireplace."

He produced a glass tube which had once contained bath salts, and which had been in his pocket for some time in case it should come in useful.

"Hold this, Lorna."

Lorna held it over the cream tiles of the hearth, while Jock raised the lever of his pen. Out spurted a high jet of ink, and dropped on the tiles. Quickly Jock snapped the lever, and out rushed more ink. The children stared at it in dismay. They didn't want Aunt Lucy to come in and see it there, and discover that they had tried to fill Lorna's pen after all, and had made such a bad job of it.

"Where's your hanky?" demanded Jock in a low voice.

"It isn't mine, it's one of Mother's, and she'll be rather cross if I make it all inky," said Lorna.

"Well, I'll use mine, but you'll have to lend me yours at tea-time, for I've got an awful cold," said Jock.

There was a soft shuffle on the mat. Lorna looked and gasped, as the crack of the just open door became wider and with a joyful snort, in sidled the blotting-paper dog.

"He must have followed the car!" she exclaimed. "How did he find out where it was going - it must have been out of sight in a minute. Isn't he rather clever, Jock?"

"S-s-sh!" whispered Jock. "Come here, BP. Come on old

chap,"

Up came BP, shaking his head and dancing with excitement. Jock pushed him gently against the fender-stool and he very carefully mopped up the ink with his white tail, which became as blotched and smudgy as the rest of his body. Then he rolled him over on his back and polished up the tiles until not a trace of the spill was left.

"Now we must put him out," he said, "or he'll roll on a rug or thump that tail on a cushion, and that'll be far worse than the big blot on the hearth."

They lifted him up between them so that the inky tail didn't come near them, and put him in the garden. When Lorna saw how terribly disappointed he looked she felt quite sad, and she now knew for certain how much she liked the blotting-paper dog. They told him to go home, but he went only a very little way, and sat among the shrubs till the car should start once more.

"I hope he won't get in," said Lorna nervously. "I hope he'll have the sense to stay where he is."

And he had. He got home late that evening, an hour and a half after Lorna had come in. Just after his arrival Jock rang the bell.

"Here!" said he, holding out a pink packet. "I bought this with some of my birthday money."

"What is it?" said Lorna.

"A shampoo powder for BP. If you use it you won't have to rub him until it hurts. Have you washed him yet?"

"No. He's only just in. I'm going to do him now. But I could have managed with soap, Jock. You shouldn't have wasted a shampoo powder on him."

"It isn't a waste." said Jock. "He's a good dog, who's there at the right moment and he deserves it."

LITTLE LORD FAUNTLEROY An Extract

Frances Hodgson Burnett

*Cedric has been summoned from America to live with his
grandfather, Lord Dorincourt, in England and assume his rightful
title, Little Lord Fauntleroy. He is just eleven years old and he
and his Grandfather develop a very special relationship. In this
extract Cedric is learning to ride.*

Lord Dorincourt had occasion to wear his grim smile many a
time as the days passed by. Indeed, as his acquaintance with his
grandson progressed, he wore the smile so often that there were
moments when it almost lost its grimness. There is no denying
that before Lord Fauntleroy had appeared on the scene the old
man had been growing very tired of his loneliness and his gout
and his seventy years.

The morning the new pony had been tried by Little Lord
Fauntleroy, the Earl had been so pleased that he had almost
forgotten his gout. When the groom had brought out the
pretty creature, which arched its brown glossy neck and tossed
its fine head in the sun, the Earl had sat at the open window of
the library and had looked on while Fauntleroy took his first
riding lesson. He wondered if the boy would show signs of
timidity. It was not a very small pony, and he had often seen
children lose courage in making their first attempt at riding.

Fauntleroy mounted in great delight. He had never been on a
pony before, and he was in the highest spirits. Wilkins, the
groom, led the animal by the bridle up and down before the
library window.

"He's a well plucked 'un he is," Wilkins remarked in the
stable afterwards with many grins. "It weren't no trouble to put
him up. An old 'un wouldn't ha' sat any straighter when he
were up. He ses – ses he to me, 'Wilkins,' he ses, 'am I sitting up
straight? They sit up straight at the circus,' ses he. And I ses, 'As
straight as a arrer, your lordship!' and he laughs as pleased as
could be, and he ses 'That's right,' he ses 'you tell me if I don't
sit up straight, Wilkins'."

74

But sitting up straight and being led at a walk were not altogether and completely satisfactory. After a few minutes Fauntleroy spoke to his grandfather – watching him from the window.

"Can't I go by myself?" he asked. "And can't I go faster? The boy on Fifth Avenue used to trot and canter!"

"Do you think you could trot and canter?" said the Earl.

"I should like to try," answered Fauntleroy.

His Lordship made a sign to Wilkins, who at the signal brought up his own horse and mounted it and took Fauntleroy's pony by the leading rein.

"Now," said the Earl, "Let him trot."

The next few minutes were rather exciting to the small equestrian. He found that trotting was not so easy as walking, and the faster the pony trotted, the less easy it was.

"It j-jolts a g-goo-good deal – do-doesn't it?" he said to Wilkins. "D-does it j-jolt y-you?"

"No, my lord," answered Wilkins. "You'll get used to it in time. Rise in your stirrups."

"I'm ri-rising all the t-time," said Fauntleroy.

He was both rising and falling rather uncomfortably and with many shakes and bounces. He was out of breath and his face grew red, but he held on with all his might, and sat as straight as he could. The Earl could see that from his window. When the riders came back within speaking distance, after they had been hidden by the trees a few minutes, Fauntleroy's hat was off, his cheeks were like poppies, and his lips were set, but he was still trotting manfully.

"Stop a minute!" said his grandfather. "Where's your hat?" Wilkins touched his. "It fell off, your lordship," he said with evident enjoyment. "Wouldn't let me stop to pick it up, my lord."

"Not much afraid, is he?" asked the Earl dryly.

"Him, your Lordship!" exclaimed Wilkins. "I shouldn't say as he knowed what it meant. I've taught your gentlemen to ride afore, and I never see one stick on more determiner."

"Tired?" said the Earl to Fauntleroy. "Want to get off?"

"It jolts you more than you think it will," admitted his young lordship frankly. "And it tires you a little too; but I don't want to get off. I want to learn how. As soon as I've got my breath I want to go back for the hat."

The cleverest person in the world, if he had undertaken to teach Fauntleroy how to please the old man who watched him, could not have taught him anything which would have succeeded better. As the pony trotted off again towards the avenue, a faint colour crept up in the fierce old face and the eyes, under the shaggy brows, gleamed with a pleasure such as his Lordship had scarcely expected to know again. And he sat and watched quite eagerly until the sound of the horses' hoofs returned. When they did come, which was after some time, they came at a faster pace. Fauntleroy's hat was still off. Wilkins was carrying it for him; his cheeks were redder than before, and his hair was flying about his ears, but he came at quite a brisk canter.

"There," he panted as they drew up, "I c–cantered, I didn't do it as well as the boy on Fifth Avenue, but I did it, and I stayed on!"

He and Wilkins and the pony were close friends after that. Scarcely a day passed on which the country people did not see them out together, cantering on the high road or through the green lanes. The children in the cottages would run to the door to look at the proud little brown pony with the gallant little figure sitting so straight in the saddle, and the young lord would snatch off his cap and swing it at them, and shout, "Hallo! Good morning!" in a very unlordly manner, though with great heartiness. Sometimes he would stop and talk with the children, and once Wilkins came back to the Castle with a story of how Fauntleroy had insisted on dismounting near the village school, so that a boy who was lame and tired might ride home on his pony.

"An' I'm blessed," said Wilkins, in telling the story at the stables, "I'm blessed if he'd hear of anything else! He wouldn't let me get down, because he said the boy mightn't feel comfortable on a big horse. An' ses he, 'Wilkins,' ses he, 'That boy's lame and I'm not, and I want to talk to him too.' And up the lad has to get, and my lord trudges alongside of him with his hands in his pockets, and his cap on the back of his head, a-whistling and talking as easy as you please! And when we come to the cottage, an' the boy's mother come out all in a taking to see what's up, he whips off his cap an' ses he, 'I've brought your son home, ma'am,' ses he, 'because his leg hurt him, and I don't think that stick is enough for him to lean on; and I'm going to ask my grandfather to have a pair of crutches made for him.' An' I'm blest if the woman wasn't struck all of a heap, as well she might be!"

When the Earl heard the story he was not angry, as Wilkins had been half afraid that he would be; on the contrary, he laughed outright, and called Fauntleroy up to him, and made him tell all about the matter from beginning to end, and then he laughed again. And actually, a few days later, the Dorincourt carriage stopped in the green lane before the cottage where the lame boy lived, and Fauntleroy jumped out and walked up to the door, carrying a pair of strong, light, new crutches, shouldered like a gun, and presented them to Mrs Hartle with these words: "My grandfather's compliments, and if you please, these are for your boy, and we hope he will get better."

"I said your compliments," he explained to the Earl when he returned to the carriage. "You didn't tell me to, but I thought perhaps you forgot. That was right, wasn't it?"

And the Earl laughed again, and did not say it was not.

RODDY AND SCUTTLE An Extract
Nance Paul and Eleanor Helme

Roddy has just moved to the country with his parents and experiences the joys of living near a farm for the first time especially when he gets himself a puppy.

One day, about a week after they had come to Hedlesdon, Mrs Wetherby suggested that they should walk across to the farm the other side of the common, and find out if they could be supplied with eggs and milk from there instead of buying them in the village. When lunch was over Roddy and she started out. It was quite difficult to know where the garden ended and the common began. Round the house itself there were some big beds where wallflowers and forget-me-nots and polyanthus and all sorts of spring flowers were coming out. Then there was the lawn with bulbs growing in the grass, and then down at the bottom were a few Scotch firs and a tangle of silver birch trees just putting out their first leaves. Beneath them was heather and soft squashy ground full of mosses, and a little stream which wandered away out of the garden and across the common under a low wooden bridge. The common itself was a rolling sea of heather and bracken, brown now, with narrow bright green paths trodden by the rabbits, and grassy hollows where young birch trees grew.

It was a beautiful afternoon, with billowy white clouds in a deep blue sky, and as they walked along beside the hedge which bordered their side of the common they found a root of primroses in bloom, and saw the rooks busy with twigs in the elms above. Presently the path left the hedge and took them across the open common, until finally the heather stopped and they were on a flat expanse of turf close-nibbled by a flock of geese. Beyond this stood a red-tiled farm house screened by a hedge of lilacs.

The largest of the geese came towards them with outstretched neck and much hissing. "I don't think I like him," said Roddy. "Do they always hiss like that?"

"Pretty often," said Mrs Wetherby. "But it doesn't mean anything. He's an awful old coward. Just wave your arms at him like that and he'll fly, and then turn round again and hiss and pretend he's ever so brave. Go along, you old silly!" And she and Roddy waved their arms and the whole family waddled away in high indignation.

After passing the geese they came to a pair of goats tethered, and then they went in at a gate in the hedge and up to the wooden porch of the farm house itself, through a rambling garden where daffodils were pushing up out of the grass under the apple trees. Coming round the corner of the house was Mrs Cooper, the farmer's wife, with a dish of eggs in her hand.

Mrs Wetherby explained who they were and what she had come for, and Mrs Cooper took them into the big kitchen so that she could put some of the eggs into a basket ready for them to take back at once. As they opened the door there was a gruff bark from the corner of the room, and a black, white and tan terrier ran towards them.

The gruff bark had only been to show that she was on guard. First she wagged her tail at Mrs Cooper; then she put one white paw on Mrs Wetherby's foot; and then she wriggled her whole black and white and tan body in an ecstatic welcome to Roddy. She was anything but handsome, and it would have been quite hard to say what sort of a terrier she really was. But she had great soft brown eyes, when you could get a glimpse of them under the shaggy black and tan of her head, her ears flopped over at a most becoming angle, even if they would not have pleased a judge at a show, and Roddy felt at once that he could spend the rest of the afternoon quite happily sitting on the floor and hugging her. He was sure she would understand every word he said to her.

"Oh, you darling!" was what he did say, and then sat down on the floor with her in his arms.

"That's Scurry," said Mrs Cooper. "Just you look in this

box."

Little yappings and scrabblings came from the box in the corner, and when Roddy got up and looked into it, he saw three fat puppies waddling about in the straw. When they caught sight of him they stopped biting each other's toes. The biggest of them stood still for a minute with his four legs planted squarely and stared at Roddy with his cheeky head on one side, and then gave an absurd little puppyish bark. He was just like his mother, with a very woolly black-and-tan coat, and a beautiful white shirt front and white paws.

"Why, that's the most grown-up bark he's ever given," said Mrs Cooper. "Here, you little mischiefs, come out, all three of you." She picked up the three puppies and put the big one into Roddy's arms. The two smaller ones were certainly prettier than he, but Roddy hardly had eyes for them, sitting demurely a little way off.

"They are sweet," said Roddy. "But oh, isn't this a wonderful little fellow? Look at the way he's trying to bite me!"

He sat down on the floor again, and the puppy wriggled out of his arms, pawed at him with large fat paws, and then rolled over on his back with a squeal of joy.

"Oh!" said Roddy, as the puppy stuck his little sharp teeth into his leg. "Doesn't he prick!"

Roddy would have played with the puppies all afternoon, but Mrs Cooper suggested presently that they should come out and see the calves and an early brood of chickens, and he rather reluctantly lifted the puppies back into their box. No sooner had he put them in than the big one was out again, and they all had to make a run for the door and shut it quickly behind them to prevent his following them out.

"He's always doing that," said Mrs Cooper. "Rare young scamp he is. I shan't be sorry when they're all gone. They're three months old now, and the little ones are going next week. But I haven't found a home for the big one yet."

"I think he's much the nicest," said Roddy, and then the puppies were driven out of his mind by the sight of two calves who were being given their afternoon feed of milk out of a bucket. The man who was holding the bucket looked up at the sight of visitors, and the calves lifted two milky noses, edged backwards and stared uneasily at Roddy. Then one of them put out a black tongue and licked the milk off its nose.

"Why, he's got a black tongue," said Roddy in amazement. "Dogs have pink ones, and horses."

The man laughed. "Most calves have got pink ones too," he said. "But these are Jerseys. Would you like to hold this for them? Let them lick some of it off your fingers. That's what they like."

Roddy dipped his fingers into the milk and gave a laugh of surprise when he felt the calves' rough tongues. He watched them finish their meal, and then Mrs Cooper showed him the chickens, some of them running about in the coop, one sitting on the back of the old mother-hen whilst one or two tiny yellow heads peeped out from under her breast as she clucked gently to them. He gazed at the hen and chickens, he gazed at the calves, and he thought of the puppies. They he drew a deep breath and turned to his mother. "Aren't things just perfect?" he said.

"Yes, I should think they are," she said. "And isn't it luck to have a lovely farm like this so close to us? Perhaps Mrs Cooper will let us come again sometimes."

"I suppose I couldn't always come and get the eggs?" said Roddy. "I wouldn't break them, I promise. Then I'd see those puppies again."

"Anyway, you come in and have another look at them now," said Mrs Cooper, adding as she opened the kitchen door, "I wonder what they're up to. They're very quiet."

Scurry got up in the box and wagged her tail at them, but she did not jump out, and Roddy, peering in, saw the two smaller puppies fast asleep, one with his little round bullet-head pillowed on the fat side of his brother. The big one was nowhere to be seen.

"Oh where's the other?" cried Roddy. "We did shut the door, didn't we? He can't have got lost."

"Somewhere he shouldn't be, I'll be bound," said Mrs Cooper.

"Why, there he is," said Mrs Wetherby, pointing to the coal-scuttle. There was a scrabble, and several lumps of coal fell out on the floor, and there, one large chunk grasped in his sharp white teeth, his white paws and shirt front no longer white, was the largest puppy.

"Well, I never!" said Mrs Cooper. "That's what he loves to do. Here, you naughty little rascal, what did I tell you? Nobody'll want you if you go doing things like that." All the same she gave a kiss to the top of his grimy head as she picked him up.

"May I hold him?" said Roddy, putting out his arms. The puppy squirmed gleefully, dropped the piece of coal he was still chewing, gave Roddy's chin several excited kisses, and then struggled down again for a fresh game with the piece of coal. Roddy took it from him and threw it across the room. The puppy scampered after it, tumbling over his own fat feet in his hurry. Roddy grabbed it again; so did the puppy, uttering fierce growls, and the game went on until Mrs Wetherby had to suggest that they really were making rather a mess for Mrs Cooper to clear up, and that they ought to be going.

"Oh must we?" said Roddy, who did not want this afternoon at the farm to end.

An idea seized Mrs Wetherby. "Mrs Cooper, is it true that you haven't got a home for that puppy, and you want one? I don't know what you're asking for him, but ..." She turned to Roddy. "Roddy, what would you say to having him for your very own?"

"Mother!" said Roddy. "Could I? Could somebody give him me? And you wouldn't mind, supposing he got in the coal and spilt it on the carpet, and if he should eat things?"

"Mind!" said Mrs Wetherby. "I love puppies, and you can't expect them not to do things like that. We'll go right home now, this minute Roddy, and see what Dad has to say about it. You could add him to the next bill with the eggs and things, couldn't you, Mrs Cooper, if we have him? We'll let you know tomorrow."

"Oh, let's get home as quick as ever we can," said Roddy, putting down the puppy. "Thanks most awfully for showing me everything," he added to Mrs Cooper. "And you won't let anybody else have him before we come back, will you?"

"No fear," said Mrs Cooper. "We'll wait for you, won't we, you rascal?" And she picked up the puppy, who lurched in her arms towards Roddy and nearly took a headlong somersault into the coal-scuttle again.

Roddy and his mother set off as fast as they could go across the common. The geese hissed at them again, but Roddy was chattering so hard about the puppy that he never heeded them, and when they caught sight of Mr Wetherby down under the fir trees at the bottom of the garden with Jane and Jill, both he and his mother broke into a run. They did not want to waste a minute before knowing whether Roddy really might have the puppy.

"Oh Dad," panted Roddy, "we've had the most glorious afternoon. There's all sorts of lovely things at the farm. And there's three puppies, and the biggest hasn't got a home, and may I have him? Mother says I may."

"A puppy?" said Mr Wetherby. "Just exactly what we do want here. I can't bear a house without a dog. And he's to be yours, Roddy, is he?"

"Well," said Roddy. "Mother did say ..." He paused. It did seem almost too good to be true.

His father put his hands on his shoulders and laughed. "Of course he shall be yours, old man. What sort of a dog is he?" he asked Mrs Wetherby.

"M'm ..." she said. "I don't think I should really like to say. But the mother's a darling; just the dear sort of nothing-in-particular I love."

"What kind of size?" asked Mr Wetherby.

"Well, terrier size, fairly big, and rather fluffy, and black and white and tan. Oh you know what I mean. You couldn't say 'No' if you saw her and the pups."

"I'm don't want to say No," said Mr Wetherby. "Right you are, Roddy, you shall be the first of the family to own a bit of livestock over here. Mind you take good care of him, and don't let him get into more mischief than you can help."

"I expect he is rather naughty about coal," said Roddy solemnly.

As he spoke there was a loud wail behind them. Jane and Jill, the twins, had grown tired of the fir cones which Mr Wetherby had been building into a castle for them. But when Jill swept the whole heap into the stream Jane thought she would like to go and fetch them out again, whereupon she sat down in the middle of the water, followed by Jill, who always had to do everything that her twin did.

"Heavens!" said Mr Wetherby. "Now I shall be catching it from Lizzie. I did ask for old clothes, but we do seem to have got in a pretty good mess, don't we?"

"Well, lucky for you Lizzie's out," said Mrs Wetherby. "Come along, Jill, you haven't hurt yourself a bit, you know. And Jane. No, you can't have those fir cones now. Roddy'll get them for you afterwards. In you come and find some dry things."

Before the twins were dry and respectable once more a caller had arrived. While Mrs Wetherby was showing her round the garden after tea Mr Wetherby went off with letters to the post, and Roddy was left to amuse the twins. They pretended they were on a boat, but all the time Roddy was thinking of the puppy. He became more sure every minute that he really could not wait till tomorrow to tell Mrs Cooper that he might have him, and when Lizzie came in he had quite made up his mind to go and fetch him at once.

He ran downstairs, meaning to ask his mother to go with him, but she and the caller were still deep in the discussion of rock plants and he did not like to interrupt. So, after a moment's hesitation, off he went by himself, across the stream and through the birch trees, away out over the common, where the sun was setting behind the line of elm trees. It seemed quite a long way with nobody to talk to, and the light was going fast by the time he neared the farm. An owl startled him terribly by flying noiselessly in front of him, and he was even more startled when the soft white shape gave vent to a most eerie shriek just after it had passed him. He trudged steadily on, though, comforting himself with the thought that he knew all about how to frighten the geese off if they should still be awake. What he was not prepared for was one of the goats, who appeared suddenly behind a gorse bush and ran at him with her head down. It was only her idea of play, but it was not quite Roddy's when she butted him firmly behind and knocked him down in a muddy puddle. He was up again in a minute, and as he stood facing the goat, ready this time to stand fast if she should charge again, Mrs Cooper came up, leading the other one.

"Oh, she is naughty," she cried. "But it's only her bit of fun. Has she hurt you?"

"I don't think so," said Roddy. "Anyway, it doesn't matter. Please, Father's said I may have that puppy, so please may I take him away now, this minute?"

"Well, I never," said Mrs Cooper. "If that isn't quick work. And you've come all by yourself?"

"Yes," said Roddy. "There was a caller and Mother was busy, and I couldn't wait. Will he be able to walk back, and do you think he'll follow me?"

"I'd be a bit afraid of him getting lost," said Mrs Cooper. "And it'll soon be dark."

"I'll carry him then," said Roddy. "I expect I can find the way all right."

"Well, I never,"said Mrs Cooper again. "He's not going to wait till somebody helps him! But, you know, he's rather heavy," she went on to Roddy. "Just you wait a bit while I think. Look, here's the milk-float coming back, and Bert can drive you both home in that. Bert!" she called to the lad. "Half a minute. I want you to drive this young gentleman over to The Gables."

Roddy followed Mrs Cooper into the house, and there was the biggest puppy sitting amongst the coal again. He stopped chewing it as the door opened, and sat with one clumsy paw on the lump, his little forehead all wrinkled up with interest to see who was coming.

"He's always in the scuttle!" said Roddy. "I shall call him that," he added after a minute's thought. "Scuttle. Do you think that would be a nice name for him?" The puppy gave a yap, bundled out of the scuttle, and landed in a heap at Roddy's feet. "I think he's going to like me, don't you?" asked Roddy anxiously.

"I'm quite sure he will, and that's a fine name for him. Here Scurry , come and say goodbye to your son."

Scurry wagged her tail, but really seemed to take very little interest.

"Oh, I hadn't thought of that," said Roddy, his face falling for a minute. "Do you think she'll mind terribly? I'll bring him over to see her very often if you think she'd like it. Perhaps we could take her back to tea with us sometimes."

"I don't think you need worry about that," said Mrs Cooper. "Scurry's got plenty to do, what with rats and rabbits, and she'll get all the more notice herself when the puppies are gone. There now, I think you'd better sit here like that, and hold Scuttle tight. That's it, Bert, off you go."

Scurry stood at the garden gate wagging her tail, the yaps from the two puppies left behind in the kitchen grew fainter as they drove away, and Roddy found his whole attention taken up with trying to hold the wriggling puppy.

"No, Scuttle, you must sit still," he said, as the puppy made a frantic grab for the steering wheel. "Oh, that's my nose!" Scuttle, feeling himself pulled back, had turned round and seized the first thing that came handy.

"You'll have a lively time with him, you will," remarked Bert with a grin.

"I never asked Mrs Cooper what he ought to have to eat. What do you think? Oh, but my Mother's sure to know."

"Bit of anything that's going, I expect," said Bert.

"Why, he's gone to sleep," said Roddy, after a few minutes.

"Pups are like that," said Bert. "One minute they're chewing you up, the next sleeping so sound you can't wake them. This is your gate, isn't it? Here you are. That's right. Good night." And Bert disappeared into the dusk.

The front door stood open and none of the curtains of the downstairs windows were drawn. Roddy could see his mother standing at the telephone, looking really worried, and heard her voice: "Number engaged? Oh dear!". She turned round and saw Roddy, with Scuttle fast asleep in his arms, the round head with its wrinkled forehead flopping over his shoulder.

"Oh Roddy boy," she cried. "That's where you've been. I was just telephoning to see if by any chance you had gone to Mrs Cooper. You really did give us a bit of a fright, you know."

"I'm very sorry," said Roddy, opening his eyes very wide.

"I didn't think of that. You see, I was so afraid perhaps somebody else would come and want Scuttle before the morning, and I couldn't ask you because of that lady."

"Is Scuttle what you're going to call him?" asked Mrs Wetherby. "Was he in the coal-scuttle again? Well, that's a very good name for him. But now we must just find Dad and Lizzie. They're both out hunting for you. I wasn't sure if you'd know the way home."

"I would have done, but Mrs Cooper thought it would be rather difficult to carry Scuttle, so Bert brought me in the milk-float."

There was a quick step outside and Mr Wetherby came in. "Hullo Roddy, there you are. That's all right then. And who on earth's this? Looks a jolly little beggar."

"That's Scuttle," said Roddy. "I've been to fetch him. He's very sleepy, but perhaps he'll wake up now."

That was exactly what Scuttle did, suddenly and with no warning. Up he sat in Roddy's arms, gave a large yawn which ended in a very small bark, put his head on one side, and looked enquiringly at Mr Wetherby.

"Hullo, young sir," said he, tickling the puppy behind his soft ears. Scuttle twisted his head round to get the full benefit of the tickling, and nearly rolled out of Roddy's arms. Roddy sat down with a plump in the nearest chair, whence Scuttle took a flying bound on to the floor, fell over, picked himself up, and seized hold of Mr Wetherby's leather shoe-lace. "Oh, he's learnt to like leather already, has he? Tomorrow we'll go to the cobbler's and get him a real good chunk of it, so that he can chew that instead of running off with all our shoes. However, the first thing is, where's he going to sleep?"

"If you'd find him a box, or knock one up for him, he'd be quite all right in this little cool green-house off the sitting room," said Mrs Wetherby. "He'll probably howl at first but that can't be helped. Oh, Scuttle, you really are a little love," she said, going down on her knees and letting the puppy bite first at her fingers and then at the buttons on her jersey and back again at her fingers.

"I wonder what Jane and Jill will say to him," said Roddy. "I suppose they're in bed now. I do want him to be a surprise for them. They won't hear him before I can get up in the morning and show him them, will they?"

"That depends on how early you're up, son," said Mr Wetherby. "Meantime, supposing you go and get a saucer of bread and milk for him while I find a box."

Roddy trotted off with Scuttle lurching after him and making vain attempts to bite his heels.

Mr and Mrs Wetherby looked at each other. "I suppose he oughtn't to have gone off by himself like that," she said. "But it's pretty good his having the pluck to do it – strange place, the dark and all."

It was only just growing light the next morning when Roddy woke up and for a few minutes, though he had a feeling something lovely had happened, he could not quite remember what it was. Then he did remember, and sat up in bed to listen. Not a sound came from the green-house below. He jumped up and put his head out of the window to hear if Scuttle was stirring, and then decided hurriedly that it was most strange for him to be so quiet. Could he have got out? Was anything the matter? Roddy felt that he must make sure at once. He ran along the passage and downstairs, through the sitting room and into the green house. The sound of the opening door roused Scuttle, and by the time Roddy reached the box he was standing up on his hind legs, craning out.

"Did you think I was never coming, Scuttle?" said Roddy. "Are you very tired of being shut up?" He opened the garden door and looked out, while Scuttle whined and scratched eagerly at the edge of his box. Roddy came back to him and lifted him up. "It's a lovely morning," he said. "And I'm sure you'll like the garden. Would you like to see it now?"

Scuttle saw more than the garden. He saw also a pair of slippers of Mr Wetherby's lying by the door. Scrambling out of Roddy's arms he grabbed at one of them and was off over the lawn with it in triumph. "Oh! Supposing he runs away," thought Roddy, and raced after him, shouting, "Drop it, Scuttle, and come in this minute." Scuttle was much too pleased with this new game to think of coming in. He ran round and round in crazy circles, keeping always out of reach, his excited yaps rather muffled by the slipper. But at last, in an attempt to yap more loudly, he dropped his treasure, and then, as Roddy pounced on it, Mrs Wetherby's head appeared out of an upstairs window.

"Roddy! My dear, what are you doing?" she called.

"I wanted to see if Scuttle was all right," said Roddy. "I was just going to show him the garden, and he got that slipper and I couldn't catch him."

"Well, come along in yourself anyway, quick," said Mrs Wetherby. "I expect he'll follow you know." Scuttle did, and by the time they were both in the green house Mrs Wetherby was downstairs with Roddy's dressing gown. "Now, up you go, and bundle back into bed again and get warm. I'll tuck Scuttle up, and then you can come down and take him for a run before breakfast, and after breakfast we'll show him to Jane and Jill."

So Scuttle had to spend another hour in his box and Roddy in bed. Scuttle was whimpering softly to himself when Roddy came down again, and there were ecstatic tail waggings as he was lifted out of his box. He had his run in the garden and was anxious to explore the stream, but Roddy hurried him in, and ate his own breakfast very quickly so as to be ready to show him to the twins as soon as they appeared for the usual last bites of their father and mother's toast and marmalade. Nobody had told them anything about Scuttle, and when they trotted in, holding Tatters between them, and saw him on Roddy's knee on the floor, they both gave a squeal of excitement, rushed forward, tripped over the mat, and fell higgledy-piggledy on top of Roddy and Scuttle. Scuttle was delighted. He kissed Jane, he kissed Jill, he kissed Tatters. He tumbled over first one pair of fat legs and then another, with more squeals from the twins, and commanding tones from Roddy: "Scuttle, you'll scratch them. You must let them get up."

Mrs Wetherby came over from the breakfast table, separated twins and puppy, and then knelt down to introduce them more formally.

"Jane and Jill," she said, "this is Scuttle. He's rather little still, and you mustn't hurt him. Stroke him, like this, and you mustn't pick him up. Oh no Jill, you'll hurt his eyes. Would you like to give him this crust?"

Jane and Jill both took hold of the crust their mother handed them and offered it together to Scuttle, who retired under the sofa with it, putting out his nose with a little yap when it was finished as if to say, "What more?"

"Nice Scuttle," said Jane. Then she turned to Tatters. "But Jane loves Tatters best." She pressed a fat kiss to the place where his second ear ought to have been.

"Just as well, perhaps," said Mr Wetherby. "Roddy, you really mustn't let them pick him up. They might hurt him. And don't you go pulling him about an awful lot yourself; you'll make his legs go crooked. And if you do lift him, get him by the scruff of the neck and put your other hand under his hind legs, see. Here, you imp, that doesn't hurt you, does it?" he went on as he picked up Scuttle in the proper way. Scuttle made a grab at his tie.

"He does always seem to be biting things," said Roddy.

"Yes," said his mother. "You keep anything that's precious out of his way, and the sooner you get that bit of leather for him the better."

"We'll go this afternoon," said Mr Wetherby. "I've a pair of shoes to take to the cobbler, anyway."

Roddy and Scuttle spent the morning blissfully, playing with the stream in the garden, following it out on to the common, or inventing new ways of crossing the wooden bridge with the little stile at each end. You could cross it by swinging yourself along outside the railings, but Roddy found the best game was to see whether he could climb over both stiles quicker than Scuttle could crawl underneath them. They played at that till Scuttle was tired, and quite suddenly curled himself up and went fast asleep amongst the heather.

The morning had gone almost before Roddy knew it had

started, and he was surprised to see the twins and Lizzie coming in from their walk. Mrs Wetherby was busy picking flowers for the house, and the twins went after her; Roddy wandered away to see what his father was doing, and for the moment Scuttle was forgotten. So was Tatters, who had been dropped by the twins on the doorstep.

A few minutes later Roddy was back at the front door. There on the mat was Scuttle, chewing something with fiendish glee. Round Scuttle on the mat were bits of what had once been Tatters. His tail lay all by itself. His two front legs were held forlornly together by a shred of wool. His one remaining ear hung out of the corner of Scuttle's mouth. Scuttle rolled a roguish eye at Roddy and then tumbled over on his back and waved his four fat paws in the air. Tatters' paws lay still on the mat.

"Oh ...!" said Roddy. "Scuttle! How could you!" He had known that Scuttle might do various naughty things but anything so appallingly wicked as tearing up the precious and beloved Tatters had never entered his head. What should he do?

Before there was any chance of doing anything the twins staggered round the corner of the house and into the porch.

Jane was the first to catch sight of the fragments of Tatters. "Tatters!" she wailed.

"Tatters all gone!" cried Jill, and then the pair of them sat down on the mat and howled together.

"Nasty Scuttle!" screamed Jill.

"Hate Scuttle!" yelled Jane.

"Go away, Scuttle!" both shrieked at once, as Scuttle, delighted at this new entertainment, dropped the last remains of Tatters and showered kisses on them.

"Scuttle didn't mean to be naughty," said Roddy. "Please don't cry. Here's my hanky."

"Go away!" shouted Jill, and smacked Roddy's face as he bent over her.

"Oh lord," said Mr Wetherby, coming on the scene at that

instant. "Who would have a puppy!"

By this time Roddy himself was almost in tears.

"Never mind, old man," said his father. "Can't be helped, and they'll get over it." "But I'm sorry," said Roddy. "Couldn't I give them something to make up?" He ran upstairs to his own room, but his store of treasures was a very small one. A stubby pencil, a twist of string, a little black pocket-book – none of these seemed likely to console Jane and Jill for the loss of Tatters. He looked at the family of ivory elephants. It would be very hard to part with them, but he did feel responsible for Scuttle's misdoings. He took the two biggest of the family and went with them to the nursery. The sight of him was the signal for fresh roars, and as for the elephants, one of them was flung into the furthest corner of the room and Lizzie only just saved the other from the fire. Roddy took back his rejected offerings, and then a bright idea struck him. Uncle James had quite unexpectedly put two pounds into his hand when he left Ockbury. He would get a new Tatters with that.

That thought considerably cheered up an otherwise melancholy lunch-time and directly afterwards Roddy and his father, leaving Scuttle in the charge of Mrs Wetherby, went off down to the village.

They bought the piece of stout leather at the cobbler's so that Scuttle would have something to exercise his teeth upon, and then went to the toyshop. There was not a very large choice, and Roddy looked round rather hopelessly.

"I want a very nice animal, please," he said. "Because, you see, my puppy has eaten Tatters, and the twins won't stop crying."

The old lady behind the counter was all sympathy. She rummaged in a drawer; she took down boxes from the shelf. At last one of those boxes produced a white rabbit. It was very large and very fluffy; it had pink velvet linings to its ears, and very bright red eyes.

"Is it very expensive?" asked Roddy, producing two pounds from his pocket.

"Well, it was five pounds," said the old lady. "But there, I've had it in stock quite a time. I could let you have it for four."

Roddy's face fell. "I've only got two pounds," he said. "All right, Roddy, I'll pay the rest," said his father.

"I don't think I'd like that," said Roddy slowly. "I ought to have looked after Scuttle. I'd like to give the twins something all by myself. Have you got anything else?" But he still looked wistfully at the white rabbit.

"I tell you what," said Mr Wetherby. "I've been thinking you ought to have some pocket money. Would you like to have your first two weeks in advance, and put it towards paying for the rabbit?"

Roddy's face lit up. "Oh yes. That would be splendid. Thank you awfully, Dad. It would really be my present then, wouldn't it?"

"Absolutely every bit," said his father.

The white rabbit was wrapped up and carried back in triumph to The Gables. Jane and Jill, with rather red eyes, were sitting on the floor looking at a picture book with their mother. Scuttle was firmly shut in his box. At the sight of Roddy both of them opened their mouths to start howling again, but when he held out the parcel the mouths shut, and four fat hands were stretched up for it.

"Look, Jane and Jill," said Roddy. "That's from me and Scuttle. See what's inside."

In a minute the string was off, the paper unwrapped, and there was the rabbit in all his white woolliness and the glory of his pink velvet ears.

"Bunny," said Jill.

"White Bunny," said Jane. "Pink ears! Love him."

"Love Roddy," said both, and four plump arms hugged him and the bunny together.

RORY'S DAY OUT

Lilian Gask

No horse at the Depot had such an evil reputation as Rory, a thoroughbred Chestnut of whom it was said that nothing and no one could tame him. He defied bit and bridle with snorts of rage, and if a rough-rider succeeded in mounting him, ten chances to one he tossed him off within the first five minutes. Punishment moved him to sullen anger without subduing him; he appeared to be almost insensible to pain, and after the most uncompromising beating would lay his fine ears wickedly back, and kick out as joyfully as ever.

Lately his doings had been worse than usual. One of the grooms he had lamed for life by deliberately crushing his leg against a post when he could not get rid of him any other way, and a second was still in hospital with three broken ribs. Having tossed him off like a bag of flour – and he was the best rider at Woolwich! – Rory had rolled upon him. A favourite trick of his, this.

"'Tis possessed he is" growled Private Brown, a well-built young fellow who stood six feet two and was broad in proportion. He had volunteered 'to see what he could do' with the redoubtable Rory, and professed himself prepared to risk his life in getting the better of him. Nevertheless, as he afterwards owned, when he saw the job in front of him he wished himself back, safe and sound, in the barrack room.

Rory sidled round as he approached, anxious to have him comfortably within reach of his hind legs; but seeing that Brown was on his guard, he suddenly changed his tactics. Prone on the ground he flopped himself, with teeth and hoofs in readiness to repel attack. And there he lay until his enemy retired, unmoved by the proddings of sharp-pointed poles, and plainly master of the situation.

That afternoon he bit a stable orderly's shoulder, catching him unawares. Five minutes before, the man had struck him for no particular reason except that he owed him a grudge; but there was no one to plead this excuse on behalf of Rory when he was brought before the Commanding Officer. At the brief Court of Inquiry which followed he was condemned as incurably vicious, and ordered to be 'cast' – that is, sold out of His Majesty's Service.

"It's a pity," said one of the officers, a slim young fellow with lint-coloured hair, popularly known as 'The Dandy'. "He's vicious, I grant you, but he's got a fine head, and I never saw a brute with better action. If he were taken gently for a while he might give a better account of himself."

"Well, you're welcome to try your hand on him" replied the Commanding Officer, with a grim smile. Nothing loth, the Dandy stepped up to Rory and patted his nose – a liberty that had not been attempted before at the Depot.

Rory started and shied, and then stood still. He had never been more surprised in his life.

"Come along, my beauty," said the Dandy quietly, leisurely catching his halter. And Rory, looking dazed, went with him like a lamb.

By the special request of his new friend, he was now transferred to his own troop, and not a man in the ranks was not interested in the Dandy's experiment. Day after day that imperturbable soldier, his hair parted perfectly down the middle, and booted and dressed to perfection, led the fiery steed to the riding school, talking to him the while in a confidential undertone. Not a whip was allowed to come within sight, nor a single harsh word to be spoken in his hearing. He was petted and coaxed, and called endearing names; and however stubborn he might be at first he usually ended by doing what he was told.

At this point he was given a handful of corn, which he accepted with obvious pleasure; and presently, corn or no corn, there was nothing he would not do for this slim young officer who believed in the conquest of evil with good.

It was a proud moment for the Dandy when Rory, his education completed, stood with perfect docility for him to mount, and then carried him to the head of his troop as if he had been the king. To watch the way in which the thoroughbred moved was a delight to anyone who loved horses, and when, his rider having dismounted, he tucked his nose into his pocket for sugar, the men gave him a round of applause. Rory acknowledged the ovation with a friendly whinny, albeit with an air of surprise. And from this time forward he never showed the slightest sign of vice.

His army days came to an end at last owing to the inevitable approach of age, and, with an unblemished character, he was discharged and sold. His purchaser was a frail old Minister whose legs refused to carry him any longer when he visited his scattered flock. Rory might have served him ill had he been less gentle, for he was full of fierce misery at the loss of his friends; but though he eyed his new master disdainfully, the kindliness of the old man's voice disarmed his gathering wrath.

The two got on very well together, for Rory had learnt to be patient. The Minister did not 'ride' him, he merely sat on his back; and Rory, with what seemed like tolerant pity for his infirmities, accommodated his pace to suit him. Now and then he looked over his shoulder as if to ask, "Am I going too fast for you?" and when they came to a rough bit of road he always slackened his pace.

Towards the close of an autumn afternoon, when the wind blew chill and the upward path was slippery with rain, Rory found it very difficult to tread firmly on the wet clay. A slight swerve on his part, and the minister rolled off; he fell quite comfortably, and was not hurt, but one foot was caught in the stirrup, and refused to be shaken free. Rory twisted himself into all sorts of attitudes to try to release him, but in the stirrup that unfortunate foot remained.

"We must wait, Rory," said the Minister presently, his tranquillity undisturbed. "Someone may come home this way from market."

Rory snorted his scorn of such a feeble comfort – who would willingly cross the hills after dusk? He wanted his stall, and his evening meal, but he was also troubled at his masters's plight. He knew it wasn't right he should lie there in the wet, and each moment now it was growing darker.

The wind moaned wearily through the pines that skirted the side of the road, and from the distance came the ringing of church bells. The Minister smiled as he listened.

"The evening brings a ' hame'," he quoted, and he moved his head that he might listen. As he did so, Rory caught the brim of his wide felt hat between his teeth, and tried to raise him. The hat, as was only expected, came off in his lips, but Rory was not yet baffled. He had 'got his hand in', so to speak, and knew what he would do next.

"Let be, good creature" cried the old man feebly. "You can do no good – I must stay where I am!" The next moment he felt his collar firmly gripped, and Rory had lifted him off the ground.

To raise ten stone, and a dead weight at that, is no easy task for an old horse, but Rory did it triumphantly. He could not neigh, for his mouth was full, but when he had lifted the old man high enough for him to free his foot, he shook him gently to show his meaning. Rallying all his strength, the Minister kicked away the stirrup, and, his shoulder still held in Rory's grip, felt his legs under him once more.

Then Rory stood for him to mount, as he had stood for the slim young officer whose trust in him had saved him disgrace. Grateful, but almost too spent to wonder, the old man clasped him round the neck, and, making no pretence of finding the reins, clung there and was carried home.

His wife was anxiously awaiting him in the low white house beyond the hill; and when she had tucked him up safe in bed, smoothing back his scant locks as she whispered, "Sleep well, dear heart!" she went to the stable with a bran mash for Rory, and kissed him as if he were one of her children whom she had long since lost. Being a dumb beast, Rory knew well that the best way to comfort her when she burst into tears upon his neck was just to let her cry on, but now and then he nosed her hand, to show that he understood.

That had been the old Minister's last ride, for he slept so well that he did not wake. Rory missed his voice, but he too was growing old, and his strongest affections were in the past. Though he did not know, there was much discussion as to what was to happen to him, but the Minister's widow was firm. "I would sooner sell all I have than part with Rory" she cried. And her married niece, who had come over to settle things up for her, knew better than to argue after this.

So Rory stayed in his homely stable, and later on it was found, to everyone's surprise, that his mistress would have money enough to buy a light cart in which she could drive him. She had never 'felt so fine' in all her life as when she first took him into town, and her innocent pleasure in his grand looks made her neighbours smile.

"Eh, he's a grand creature," said one good body, "but take care that he's not too much for you. Where would you be if he took it into his head to run away?"

"Sitting in my chaise, just where I am now!" returned the old dame proudly. She felt as sure of Rory as she did of her tabby cat, who had slept between the old horse's feet from the first day that he had come.

The widow had driven Rory for two years taking her cheery face and homely wisdom wherever she heard of anyone sick or sad, when the married niece sent her a new bonnet. It was black, of course, but nattily trimmed with ribbon instead of crepe, and a glittering ornament of jet held the central bow in its place.

Now Rory's mistress had once been extremely pretty, even at sixty years old her pink and white complexion might have been envied by many a girl. She looked at herself this way and that as she tied the wide strings beneath her chin, and suddenly thought it was high time that she took her second-best shawl into everyday wear. The thrush on the hawthorn sang clear and sweet, for the orchard trees were in blossom; and the little old lady began to sing too – the earth was so green and new.

"The spring has got into my head!" she said, as she replaced the new bonnet in its nest of tissue paper. And all that morning she couldn't keep still.

A daring plan came into her mind when she heard the news that the postman brought. At Debtown, not quite ten miles away, that very afternoon there was to be a grand review; and she had loved soldiers all her life.

"We'll have a lovely day out, you and I, Rory," she cried, as, in all the glory of the new bonnet, she nimbly climbed into the chaise. Rory pricked up his ears – the bright April sunshine had stirred his old blood too; and he trotted through the village at such a pace that more than one dame shook a prim grey head, and prophesied trouble to come.

The little old lady and her lordly horse caused quite a sensation when she pulled up by the common on which the troops were assembled, for Rory had never shown to more advantage. His coat still shone like polished silk, and the noble curves of his finely proportioned limbs had been untouched by age. No one could mistake him for anything but a one time Servant of the State as he stood with them at attention, and the soldiers who were nearest nudged each other. His mistress was quick to notice their admiring glances, and was humbly thankful to be wearing the new bonnet, in which she felt she did him credit.

What Rory's thoughts were no one knew, but his eyes had grown strangely alert and watchful. Soon there fell on the air a sound he knew – the bugle-call was the preparatory order for a cavalry regiment to charge. Rory threw back his head and dashed across the field; the years were forgotten – he was young once more, and that bugle-call was for him.

The officer in command was accustomed to come to quick decisions, and guessing at once why Rory had bolted, opened out his men right and left. In dashed the horse to a place in the rear, taking the correct alignment. The next order followed; the cavalry charged - so did Rory, the chaise, and his mistress. Amidst a roar of laughter, half a dozen hands were outstretched to help out the plucky old dame.

"Not a bit of it, friends!" she cried with spirit. "I am safe with Rory. I shall stay where I am."

And as she would not leave the chaise, and Rory would not leave the regiment, they all took part in the exercise. Rory still knew each bugle-call as well as the men did themselves. He charged and halted, stood to attention, and gave place, as if it were only yesterday he had been the darling of the regiment; and when the review was at last over, the Commanding Officer rode up to congratulate his beaming mistress on his achievements. "It is just his day out!" the old lady smiled, well pleased with the whole adventure.

And as Rory carried her home through the twilight, past the very spot where he had slipped on the wet clay, she wished that the Minister could have seen how well his favourite had borne himself.

THE DOG CRUSOE An Extract

R M Ballantyne

The dog Crusoe was once a pup. Now do not toss your head contemptuously and exclaim, "Of course he was; I could have told you that." You know very well that you have often seen a man above six feet high, broad and powerful as a lion, with a bronzed shaggy face and the stern glance of an eagle, of whom you have said, or thought, or heard others say, "It is scarcely possible to believe that such a man was once a squalling baby," If you had seen our hero in all the strength and majesty of full-grown doghood, you would have experienced a vague sort of surprise as we told you – as we now repeat – that the dog Crusoe was once a pup – a soft, round, sprawling, squeaking pup, as fat as a tallow candle, and as blind as a bat.

But we draw particular attention to the fact of Crusoe's having once been a pup, because in connection with the days of his puppyhood there hangs a tale. This peculiar dog may thus be said to have had two tails – one in connection with his body, the other with his career. This tale, though short, is very harrowing, and as it is intimately connected with Crusoe's subsequent history we will relate it here. But before doing so we must beg our reader to accompany us beyond the civilized portions of the USA – beyond the frontier settlements of the 'far west', into those wild prairies which are watered by the great Missouri River – the Father of Waters – and his numerous tributaries.

Here dwell the Pawnees, the Sioux, the Delawares, the Crows, the Blackfeet, and many other tribes of Red Indians, who are gradually retreating step by step towards the Rocky Mountains, as the advancing white man cuts down their trees and ploughs up their prairies. Here, too, dwell the wild horse and the wild ass, the deer, the buffalo, and the badger; all, men and brutes alike, wild as the power of untamed and ungovernable passion can make them, and free as the wind that sweeps over their mighty plains. There is a romantic and exquisitely beautiful spot on the banks of one of the tributaries above referred to - a long stretch of mingled woodland and meadow, with a magnificent lake lying like a gem in its green bosom - which goes by the name of the Mustang Valley. This remote vale is but thinly peopled by white men, and is still a frontier settlement round which the wolf and the bear prowl curiously and from which the startled deer bounds terrified away. At the period of which we write, the valley had just been taken possession of by several families of squatters, who, tired of the turmoil and the squabbles of the ten frontier settlements, had pushed boldly into the far west to seek a new home for themselves, where they could have "elbow room," regardless alike of the dangers they might encounter in unknown lands and of the Redskins who dwelt there.

The newcomers gave one satisfied glance at their future home, and then set to work to erect log huts. Soon the axe was heard ringing through the forests, and tree after tree fell to the ground, while the occasional sharp ring of a rifle told that the hunters were catering successfully for the camp. In course of time the Mustang Valley began to assume the aspect of a thriving settlement, with cottages and waving fields clustered together in the midst of it.

Of course the savages soon found it out and paid it occasional visits. These dark-skinned tenants of the woods brought furs of wild animals with them, which they exchanged with the white men for knives, and beads, and baubles and trinkets of brass and tin. But they hated the "Pale-faces" with bitter hatred, because their encroachments had at this time lessened the extent of their hunting grounds, and nothing but the numbers and known courage of the squatters prevented these savages from butchering and scalping them all.

The leader of this band of pioneers was a Major Hope, a gentleman whose love for nature in its wildest aspects determined him to exchange barrack life for a life in the woods. The Major was a first-rate shot, a bold, fearless man, and an enthusiastic naturalist. He was past the prime of life, and, being a bachelor, was unencumbered with a family. His first act on reaching the site of the new settlement was to start building a block house, to which the people might retire in case of a general attack by the Indians.

In this block house Major Hope took up his abode as the guardian of the settlement. And here the dog Crusoe was born; here he sprawled in the early morn of life; here he leaped, and yelped and wagged his shaggy tail in the excessive glee of puppyhood; and from the wooden portals of this blockhouse he bounded forth to the chase in all the fire, and strength and majesty of full-grown doghood.

Crusoe's father and mother were magnificent Newfoundlanders. There was no doubt as to their being of the genuine breed, for Major Hope had received them as a parting gift from a brother officer, who had brought them both from Newfoundland itself. The father's name was Crusoe, the mother's name was Fan. Why the father had been so called no one could tell. The man from whom Major Hope's friend had obtained the pair was a poor illiterate fisherman, who had never heard of the celebrated "Robinson" in all his life. All he knew was that Fan had been named after his own wife. As for Crusoe, he had got him from a friend, who had got him from another friend, whose cousin had received him as a marriage-gift from a friend of his; and that each had said to the other that the dog's name was "Crusoe," without reasons being asked or given on either side. On arriving at New York the Major's friend, as we have said, made him a present of the dogs. Not being much of a dog fancier, he soon tired of old Crusoe, and gave him away to a gentleman, who took him down to Florida, and that was the end of him. He was never heard of again.

When Crusoe, junior, was born, he was born, of course, without a name. That was given to him afterwards in honour of his father. He was also born in company with a brother and two sisters, all of whom drowned themselves accidentally, in the first month of their existence, by falling into the river which flowed past the blockhouse – a calamity which occurred, doubtless, in consequence of their having gone out without their mother's leave. Little Crusoe was with his brother and sisters at the time, and fell in along with them, but was saved from sharing their fate by his mother who, seeing what had happened, dashed with an agonized howl into the water, and seizing him in her mouth brought him ashore in a half-drowned condition. She afterwards brought the others ashore one by one, but the poor little things were dead.

And now we come to the harrowing part of our tale.

One beautiful afternoon, in that charming season of the American year called the Indian summer, there came a family of Sioux Indians to the Mustang Valley, and pitched their tent close to the blockhouse. A young hunter stood leaning against the gate-post of the palisades, watching the movements of the Indians, who, having just finished a long talk with Major Hope, were now in the act of preparing supper. A fire had been kindled on the green sward in front of the tent, and above it stood a tripod, from which hung a large tin camp-kettle. Over this stood an ill-favoured Indian woman, or squaw, who, besides attending to the contents of the pot, bestowed sundry cuffs and kicks upon her little child, which sat near to her playing with several Indian curs that gambolled round the fire. The master of the family and his two sons reclined on buffalo robes, smoking their stone pipes in silence. There was nothing peculiar in their appearance. Their faces were neither dignified nor coarse in expression, but wore an aspect of stupid apathy, which formed a striking contrast to the countenance of the young hunter, who seemed an amused spectator of their proceedings.

The youth referred to was very unlike, in many respects, to what we are accustomed to suppose a backwoods' hunter should be. He did not possess that quiet gravity and staid demeanour which often characterise these men. True, he was tall and strongly made, but no one would have called him stalwart, and his frame indicated grace and agility rather than strength. But the point about him which rendered him different from his companions was his bounding, irrepressible flow of spirits, strangely coupled with an intense love of solitary wandering in the woods. None seemed so well fitted for social enjoyment as he; none laughed so heartily or expressed such glee in his mischief-loving eye; yet for days together he went off alone into the forest, and wandered where his fancy led him, as grave and silent as an Indian warrior.

After all, there was nothing mysterious in this. The boy followed implicitly the dictates of nature within him. He was amiable, straightforward, and intensely earnest. When he laughed he let it out, as sailors have it, "with a will." When there was good cause to be grave, no power on earth could make him smile. We have called him boy, but in truth he was about that uncertain period of life when a youth is said to be neither a man nor a boy. His face was good-looking and masculine; his hair was reddish-brown and his eyes bright blue. He was costumed in the deerskin cap, leggings, moccasins and shirt common to the west hunter.

"You seem tickled with the Injuns, Dick Varley," said a man who at that moment came from the blockhouse.

"That's just what I am, Joe Blunt," replied the youth, turning with a broad grin to his companion.

"Have a care, lad; do not laugh at them too much. They soon take offence; and them Redskins never forgive."

"But I'm only laughing at the baby," returned the youth, pointing to the child, which, with a mixture of boldness and timidity, was playing with a pup, wrinkling up its fat face into a smile when its playmate rushed away in sport, and opening wide its jet-black eyes in grave anxiety as the pup returned at full gallop.

"It 'ud make an owl laugh," continued young Varley, "to see such an odd picture of itself."

He paused suddenly, and a dark frown covered his face as he saw the Indian woman stoop quickly down, catch the pup by its hind-leg with one hand, seize a heavy piece of wood with the other, and strike violent blows on the throat. Without taking the trouble to kill the poor animal outright the savage then held its still writhing body over the fire, in order to singe off the hair before putting it into the pot to be cooked.

The cruel act drew young Varley's attention more closely to the pup, and it flashed across his mind that this could be no other than young Crusoe, which neither he nor his companion had seen before, although they had often heard others speak of and describe it.

Had the little creature been one of the unfortunate Indian curs, the two hunters would probably have turned from the sickening sight with disgust, feeling that, however much they might dislike such cruelty, it would be of no use attempting to interfere with Indian customs. But the instant the idea that it was Crusoe occurred to Varley he uttered a yell of anger, and sprang towards the woman with a bound that caused the three Indians to leap to their feet and grasp their tomahawks.

Blunt did not move from the gate, but threw forward his rifle with a careless motion, but an expressive glance, that caused the Indians to resume their seats and pipes with an emphatic "Wah!" of disgust at having been startled by such a trifle; while Dick Varley snatched poor Crusoe from his dangerous and painful position, scowled angrily in the woman's face, and turning on his heel, walked up to the house, holding the pup tenderly in his arms.

Joe Blunt gazed after his friend with a grave, solemn expression till he disappeared; then he looked at the ground, and shook his head.

Poor Crusoe was singed almost naked, his wretched tail seemed little better than a piece of wire filed off to a point, and he vented his misery in piteous squeaks as the sympathetic Varley confided him tenderly to the care of his mother. How Fan managed to cure him no one can tell, but cure him she did, for in the course of a few weeks, Crusoe was as well and sleek and fat as ever.

A HORRIBLY HORSEY DAUGHTER

Josephine Pullein-Thompson

It was going to be a dull weekend, thought Miranda Cummings. Prep, television, books from the library, but nothing really to do, except for her ride, one hour on Saturday morning. Now, if she had a pony of her own ... But it was no use wasting time on that old fantasy; for years she'd imagined herself schooling, riding perfect half-passes, seen herself in the show ring, jumping clear rounds. And there wasn't a chance of any of it coming true; it was just a stupid dream.

It wasn't as though they were poor, it wasn't as though they lived in the centre of a huge city. Their house stood in the same road as a riding school and there was plenty of room beside the garage for a loose-box, Miranda had often paced it out. No, it was simply that her father had convinced himself that horsey girls were dull, stupid and generally horrible. He could never see beautiful girls riding gracefully on Anglo-Arabs. It was always large, fat, ugly girls slumped on ponies too small for them to which he pointed triumphantly saying: "There, that's what you'd look like if I let you do all this riding." And when Miranda's mother, who was on Miranda's side, pointed out that she was really quite pretty, with long dark hair and brown eyes, and that she must be intelligent to have won a scholarship to St Catherine's, her father would answer, "Oh I'm quite contented with her as she is. It's just that I won't take the risk of her changing. I don't want a horsey daughter who talks about ponies at every meal. And anyway she's no good at it," he would add to Miranda's annoyance, for how could she improve when she only rode for one hour a week?

All the time she'd been working for the scholarship, Miranda had encouraged herself with the idea that her father might reward her with a pony, but when, delighted with the result, he'd merely taken her out to lunch at the most expensive restaurant in Cranbourne, she had given up hope. Since then she had tried not to dream of becoming a superb rider, because dreams which couldn't be realised were a waste of time, but just occasionally when there was only a dreary weekend ahead, all the old longings came back in full force. And that was how it was when Liz Holder telephoned and asked for her help.

Mr Cummings was away on business so Miranda went in search of her mother. She was arranging the dining room for her Oxfam Bring and Buy sale the next day.

'Mum, Miss Barnes has gone to Yorkshire for her niece's wedding and Anne Ashmore who was supposed to help Liz run the stables this weekend has let her down. Liz wants me to help instead; she says she's desperate, can I?"

Mrs Cummings looked undecided. "But would you be any use?" she asked. "I mean you're not very experienced yourself."

"She's asked me," answered Miranda, feeling slightly offended that her parents always thought her so useless.

"Yes, well, Dad doesn't like you hanging round the stables but this is an emergency; one must help people in trouble. Anyway, he doesn't come back from Germany until Sunday evening. Yes, that's all right, darling..."

"Oh thank you," called Miranda as she rushed back to the telephone.

Liz had said that she could manage the stable work so there was no need for Miranda to be early, but Miranda wasn't going to miss a minute of her horsey weekend and she was hurrying along the road just after eight on Saturday morning. It was a dismal-looking day. Yellow leaves drifted through the grey light and landed on the road and pavement with tiny exhausted sighs, but it wasn't raining or freezing, thought Miranda with relief ...

Liz was mucking out the three stabled horses: Stardust, Jasper and Coot. "Hullo, you're early," she said. "Well, you can fetch up the ponies as soon as Andrew and Chris come and meanwhile if you'd like to give Stardust some clean straw ..."

Miranda spread straw until Chris, who was eleven with red hair, arrived on her bicycle. Then they collected headcollars and pony nuts while they waited for Andrew. He was only nine, with blue eyes and a large face that always wore a deadpan expression; he lived opposite the stable gates.

"Miranda, if you ride one and lead one you'll be able to bring them all up in two goes," called Liz.

Most of the ponies were waiting at the field gate and they had quite a job to get the first four through without letting the whole lot out. Chris and Andrew had chosen their favourites, piebald Domino and little brown Filbert. Miranda rode Max, a stately grey of 14.2, and led Blackberry who was thickset and obstinate and no one's favourite. On the second trip Andrew chose the other little pony, Fudge, while Chris had roan Punch, and Miranda rode Rufus and led Pepsi who was Punch's twin in appearance, but not so sweet-tempered.

Liz fed the larger ponies and they groomed the smaller ones, who only had haynets, until the feeds were eaten. Then the large ones were groomed too, great clouds of dust rising from their mud-caked coats.

Miranda rode Rufus for her official ride. Liz took them in the school and gave them quite an exciting time with more jumping than Miss Barnes usually allowed. They were the best ride of the day and afterwards the standard fell steeply. When Miranda saw the eleven o'clock ride trying to put themselves up she understood why Liz had asked for her help. She was to take Clare, who was seven and had only ridden five times, on the leading rein. And besides Clare, there were two other beginners, large girls of about sixteen, who were to ride Coot and Jasper. Then there was Andrew on Filbert, a very nervous boy on Rufus, a bossy girl with huge teeth and straight hair on Blackberry and three fairly efficient-looking girls on Pepsi, Punch and Domino. Chris helped with the stirrups and held Fudge and Clare while Miranda led out Max and mounted. When Liz had checked all the girths and stirrups she mounted Stardust and led the cavalcade down the road and then along the lane towards the common. Clare was quite chatty; she said that she liked Filbert better than Fudge and that she could rise to the trot. Miranda taught her some easy points of the horse, crest and withers and knee, and told her about keeping her legs back and riding with a perpendicular stirrup leather.

Liz didn't take them over the high, open part of the common, but along the sandy tracks through the woods and presently she halted at the start of a long, grassy track and said, "If you and Clare will trot up there and wait at the top, Miranda, I'll send the people who want to canter up in ones and twos so that the ponies don't get excited."

Jean and Hazel, the large beginners, didn't want to canter, nor did the nervous boy. The bossy girl on Blackberry began to laugh at them but Liz told her to shut up and sent them all on with Miranda.

No one fell off and Andrew, who had insisted on going last, was quite sure he had galloped, though no one else thought so. Liz took the lead again and they rode along narrow, winding paths between bracken and heather and birch trees.

Clare chattered about school and Miranda taught her how to halt and to trot with folded arms. They had almost completed their circle and were waiting to cross the one busy road between them and the stables, when the bossy girl, whose name was Carol, barged past Liz and announced that there was tons of time to cross.

"Come back," shouted Liz. But Blackberry decided to carry on and as Carol tugged on the reins in the middle of the road, Liz called, "Keep them together, Miranda," and rode after Carol.

Miranda said, "Wait everyone. Stand still." And then there was a horrible crack as Blackberry lashed out. The other riders couldn't see whether it was Liz or Stardust who caught the full impact of the kick, but then Liz leaned forward, obviously in pain, and put one hand across her face. A man in a car driving past slowly shouted that she wasn't fit to be in charge of children. Miranda took over. She shepherded everyone across the road and then took Stardust's rein, for Liz seemed dazed and not in control.

"I'll be all right in a minute," she murmured. "It's just my ankle." Away from the road, Miranda dismounted and looked for the damage, but jodphurs and boot concealed whatever had happened.

"It wasn't a hard kick," said Carol. "She'll be all right."

Jean and Hazel were suggesting doctors who lived near, Andrew offered to gallop to a telephone and dial 999. Miranda came to a decision. "You go to the back," she told Carol severely, "and don't kick anyone else. Pat," she asked, "Could you lead Max? he's friends with Domino. Then I'll walk with Clare and Liz."

They walked slowly and sadly across the last stretch of the common and along the road to the stables, for they could all see that Liz was still in pain. Clare looked as though she was going to cry so Miranda had to assume a cheerful manner and explain that even if Liz's ankle was broken it would soon mend.

Chris met them at the yard gate.

"You take Clare," said Miranda. There were several mothers waiting to collect their children; the riders explained about the kick, all talking at once.

"Will you put your ponies away, please," called Miranda as the mothers crowded round her and Liz. "I think if you undo the girth you can slide the rider off with the saddle, I read about it in a book," Miranda told them.

"A splint first," said a first-aiding mother and they made one with the crook of a hunting crop under the foot and fixed it with tail bandages. Then they slid Liz off and sat her in the nervous boy's mother's car. "I'll drive her straight to the hospital," said Mrs Giles.

Miranda wrote down Liz's telephone number and promised to break the news to her mother gently and then, as the car drove away, she suddenly realised that she was in charge and alone. Well, not quite alone, Chris and Andrew would help her, but supposing anything else went wrong? She hadn't even Miss Barnes's telephone number.

"Aren't you going to book us up for next week?" asked Carol's bossy voice. "You're not very efficient, are you? I think I'd better stay and help, especially as everyone says it was my fault."

"There's no need," Miranda told her hastily. "Chris and Andrew are the regular helpers." And grabbing the diary she wrote down the names of those who were coming next week.

"I hope you'll take me again," said Clare.

The pupils gone, the ponies watered, Chris and Andrew came to her to ask about feeds; Miss Barnes always mixed them, they just took them round.

"I'll have to guess," decided Miranda. "We won't give them too many oats. They won't starve so long as they have plenty of hay and I don't want to give them colic or laminitis or get the pupils bucked off."

As soon as all the horses were munching, Miranda telephoned Liz's mother.

"An accident?" she gasped.

"Just a small one," Miranda repeated, "just her ankle and Mrs Giles has taken her to the hospital for an X-ray."

"To the hospital? Thank you, dear. I'll go down right away."

Andrew went home to lunch so it was only Miranda and Chris who ate their sandwiches in the saddle room. As she ate Miranda inspected the diary. "I'm sure Liz won't be back for days," she told Chris. "I'd better put everyone off. They won't like it if they've come miles and find no riding." But it wasn't so easy to put them off. Miss Barnes didn't bother with surnames and how could you telephone 'Jenny T' or 'David' and the one name she had written down was 'Berry'. It would waste hours, Miranda thought, ringing every Berry in the phone book.

"I should just take them," said Chris. "After all, Liz let you teach Clare. This lot aren't much good, but they're not actual beginners."

"I suppose I could take them for a hack," said Miranda. That was what she did and, though it was dull for the ponies, she took them the same ride that they had gone with Liz that morning, for it was a good safe ride with no wild gallops.

Hearing of Liz's accident, all the pupils were extra nice and helpful and when Jenny T had asked her age Miranda had hastily instructed one of the younger riders to avoid answering for she felt certain that Jenny was at least as old as she was.

Afterwards the riders of the field ponies turned them out and some offered to carry down hay and help generally so the ponies were soon fed, but everyone spilled a good deal and the yard began to look a bit of a mess.

Chris and Andrew had worked hard while the ride was out; the boxes were bedded down and the horses stabled; water and haynets were ready so, when Miranda had mixed another set of feeds, they fed the horses and gathered in the saddle room looking gloomily at the eleven dirty sets of tack.

"I have to go home at half past five," said Andrew.

"We could just wash the bits," suggested Chris. "I know Miss Barnes does sometimes when there's an emergency and this must be one."

"Yes, we'll do that," agreed Miranda and then the telephone rang and it was Liz's mother.

"We're just back from the hospital," she said. "What a palaver! They had to put her in plaster but it's only a walking one. She's broken the smaller of the two bones in the leg – her fibula. It'll be six weeks, they say, but she'll be able to get about. How are things with you? Liz's worried to death over the horses. She wants me to drive her up now, but she's not allowed to walk for twelve hours, not till the plaster dries out."

"Tell her everything is all right," answered Miranda. "Chris and Andrew have helped all day and the horses and ponies are fed etc. She needn't worry. I think we had better get in touch with Miss Barnes. It seems a pity to upset her trip and I'm sure she'll want to come home when she knows how things stand, but of course trains are few and far between on a Sunday, so if you could manage the feeding in the morning? Liz says not to worry about mess and muddle; it's just the well-being of the animals that matters."

Miranda told Chris and Andrew about the broken fibula as they washed the bits and then when they'd gone home she topped up the horses' water buckets, checked their haynets and rugs and locked the saddle room before starting on her own rather weary walk through the dusk. She felt as though years and years had passed since that morning.

"Thirty eight pounds, fifty-five pence for Oxfam," announced Mrs Cummings proudly. "Not bad was it? And how did your day go, were you able to give a helping hand?"

Miranda explained about Liz's ankle. "I'm in charge now."

"Oh poor Liz. But you can't really be in charge, darling. Not of all those horses. I mean you don't know enough and some of them are enormous. I could ring the RSPCA and ask them to send a man round."

"I know what to do," said Miranda, "And it's all done. Anyway, it's only until tomorrow and then Miss Barnes will be back. Have you had tea? I'm terribly hungry."

Much as she hated early rising Miranda was at the stables at seven-fifteen on Sunday morning. She inspected her charges; Coot, the ugly black gelding, had no water, Stardust's rug had slipped, Jasper, who'd eaten every morsel of his hay neighed indignantly for breakfast, but otherwise they seemed all right. She watered and fed them.

By the time Chris and Andrew appeared it was raining. They ran to fetch in the ponies before their coats were wet. As they mucked out and groomed, it settled down to being a wet day.

"You'll have to take the ten o'clock ride in the school," Chris told Miranda, "no one will want to go for a hack in this." They inspected the diary. Nine pupils at ten, nine at eleven.

"Some of the ten o'clock are good," said Chris.

"And some of the elevens are terrible," added Andrew. "That girl Sandra screams."

Miranda's heart was sinking. It wasn't the screaming Sandra who frightened her, but the accomplished ten o'clocks; they probably rode far better than she did. "I don't think I can take them, I'm not experienced enough," she was telling Chris when Carol's head came round the saddle room door.

"Hullo, how are you getting on? I hear Liz's leg is broken so I've come to help. I'll take a ride out."

"No you won't," answered Chris. "Miranda was put in charge and she's taking them in the school."

"Yes, that's right," Miranda was forced to agree. "And Miss Barnes has written down which ponies they are all to ride, so we only have to tack up."

"I'll saddle Stardust," said Carol, grabbing tack.

"That's Coot's bridle," Andrew told her coldly.

Miranda's feelings of inadequacy increased as the ten o'clock pupils, all looking tall and competent and quite as old as her, arrived. Chris told them of Liz's accident and how Miranda had been put in charge and Miranda unwillingly dragged her leaden legs and hollow-feeling stomach into the centre of the school, which had suddenly assumed cathedral-like proportions. She spurred herself on with the knowledge that Carol would rush forward and take over if she faltered.

The ride walked round quarrelling mildly. Peter wanted to lead and so did Fiona. Miranda said firmly that the horses were to go first and Blackberry last. With a cross sigh Peter found himself a place in the middle.

Knowing the terrible boredom of just going round and round, Miranda had thought up a full lesson. She whirled her pupils into circles and serpentines, took them from turns on the forehand and reining back into riding without stirrups. They all seemed to know the aids for everything, but Marilyn had her legs too far forward and Fiona would look down. All went well until Patsy failed to get Blackberry on the right leg and then quite suddenly everyone began to give advice, including Carol from the gallery. Above the babble Jill's voice wailed that, "Surely it was time to jump?" The other riders immediately took up the cry. Peter dismounted and prepared to carry in the jumps.

"Wait a minute," shouted Miranda above the uproar. "Blackberry is very still and shoulder-in would improve her so we're going to practise it before we jump. Who knows the aids?" To her delight no one did, so she had the ride under control and listening again. When everyone, even Blackberry, had managed to do a few steps the riders sat patting their ponies and feeling quite pleased with themselves while Andrew, Chris and Carol helped to arrange cavalletti for trotting. After that they did grid-jumping and then a twisty little course. Miranda was just presenting imaginary rosettes to the winners when a flood of eleven o'clock pupils into the gallery told her that it was time to stop.

Outside it was still raining. The second ride took over the ponies but some of the horses weren't needed. The first ride wanted to book up and the second ride needed help with its stirrups and the Alsop girls said they couldn't put their horses away because their father was waiting. Miranda was struggling with the bookings with Stardust and Jasper's reins draped round her, when down the gallery steps, helped by her mother, came Liz.

"Well done, Miranda!" she called. "That was fabulous, I couldn't have done it better myself."

"Thank you," said Miranda, still puzzling over the diary. "Is it OK if I book a friend of Patsy's for next Sunday? It'll make ten but she's small and could ride Fudge."

At that moment Sandra began to let out the most piercing screams. Her pony was stationary, but she had dropped her reins and was clinging to the pommel with both hands. Her face wore a look of terror. Miranda flung the diary at Liz and the reins of the horses to the nearest uninjured person, who, she saw with some surprise, was her own father, and rushed to Sandra's aid. "What happened? What's the matter?"

"Punch made a horrid face at Filbert," Sandra wailed tearfully, "I thought he was going to eat us."

Explaining that horses were not carnivorous and that if you hung on to your reins you could prevent their petty quarrels, Miranda led her across the yard. Order was beginning to prevail, the pupils were riding into the school, Liz had coped with the diary and Chris and Andrew were putting away the spare horses.

"I thought you weren't coming back until tonight, Dad?" said Miranda accusingly. "And I hope you don't want me because I'm terribly busy."

"So I see," said Mr Cummings. "It's all right. You carry on, my business can wait."

This was a very different ride to instruct. Some of them seemed so unsafe that Miranda didn't dare let them canter much or jump, but she organised races at the trot which were very popular. Sandra won the garden path competition, mostly because Filbert had the smallest and neatest hoofs, and announced that it was the loveliest ride she had ever had, which made up for a complaining girl who said she only liked hacking.

As they came out of the school, there was Miss Barnes looking unfamiliar in ordinary clothes.

"Oh, you're back," said Miranda, feeling suddenly deflated.

"I flew," explained Miss Barnes. "It took no time at all. Oh Miranda, you have been marvellous. I can't thank you enough. You've coped brilliantly."

Miranda stood, uncertain what to say. "Chris and Andrew did most of the work," she answered. "Now what about the ponies you don't need this afternoon, shall we turn them out?"

"No, you've done your bit and I promised your father I'd pack you off home as soon as you'd finished the lesson. I had a talk with him, but he'll tell you about that."

Miranda walked home slowly; everything seemed so flat. Prep, TV, she thought. Perhaps a hasty change into a dress, a smart lunch out. I like doing things, she thought. Her parents seemed pleased to see her.

"You really were in charge then, darling," said her mother. "Dad was most impressed. I wish I'd come along to see you in all your glory, but I was in a panic over lunch, with him turning up so unexpectedly."

"I had a talk with Miss Barnes," said Miranda's father. "She was telling me that riding offers scope at various levels: stupid people just muddle through on instinct but to the intelligent it's an art with a history and a future like any other art; quite interesting. Anyway she wants to borrow you for the next few weekends while Liz is laid up. I said you'd be delighted to help out, and after that we might think about a horse."

"A horse? Do you mean a horse for me?" asked Miranda in amazement.

"We'll think about it," said Mr Cummings, "but you'll have to promise not to become ..."

"Once I have one I'll never mention it," promised Miranda throwing her arms round him and silencing him with a smacking kiss.

LOUIS

Saki

"It would be jolly to spend Easter in Vienna this year," said Strudwarden, "and look up some of my old friends there. It's about the jolliest place I know of to be for Easter -"

"I thought we had made up our minds to spend Easter at Brighton," interrupted Lena Strudwarden, with an air of aggrieved surprise.

"You mean that you had made up your mind that we should spend Easter there," said her husband; "we spent last Easter there, and Whitsuntide as well, and the year before that we were at Worthing, and Brighton again before that. I think it would be just as well to have a real change of scene while we are about it."

"The journey to Vienna would be very expensive," said Lena.

"You are not often concerned about economy," said Strudwarden, "and in any case the trip to Vienna won't cost a bit more than the rather meaningless luncheon parties we usually give to quite meaningless acquaintances at Brighton. To escape from all that set would be a holiday in itself."

Strudwarden spoke feelingly; Lena Strudwarden maintained an equally feeling silence on that particular subject. The set that she gathered round her at Brighton and other South Coast resorts was composed of individuals who might be dull and meaningless in themselves, but who understood the art of flattering Mrs Strudwarden. She had no intention of foregoing their society and their homage and flinging herself among unappreciative strangers in a foreign capital. "You must go to Vienna alone if you are bent on going," she said; "I couldn't leave Louis behind, and a dog is always a fearful nuisance in a foreign hotel, besides all the fuss and separation of the quarantine restrictions when one comes back. Louis would die if he was parted from me for even a week. You don't know what that would mean to me." Lena stooped down and kissed the nose of the diminutive brown Pomeranian that lay, snug and irresponsive, beneath a shawl on her lap. "Look here," said Strudwarden, "this eternal Louis business is getting to be a ridiculous nuisance. Nothing can be done, no plans can be made, without some veto connected with that animal's whims or convenience being imposed. If you were a priest in attendance on some African fetish you couldn't set up a more elaborate code of restrictions. I believe you'd ask the Government to put off a General Election if you thought it would interfere with Louis's comfort in any way."

By way of answer to this tirade Mrs Strudwarden stooped down again and kissed the irresponsive brown nose. It was the action of a woman with a beautifully meek nature, who would, however, send the whole world to the stake sooner than yield an inch where she knew herself to be in the right.

"It isn't as if you were in the least bit fond of animals," went on Strudwarden, with growing irritation, "when we are down at Kerryfield you won't stir a step to take the house dogs out, even if they're dying for a run, and I don't think you've been in the stables twice in your life. You laugh at what you call the fuss that's being made over the extermination of plumage birds, and you are quite indignant with me if I interfere on behalf of an ill-treated, over-ridden animal on the road. And yet you insist on everyone's plans being made subservient to the convenience of that stupid morsel of fur and selfishness."

"You are prejudiced against my little Louis," said Lena, with a world of tender regret in her voice.

"I've never had the chance of being anything else but prejudiced against him," said Strudwarden; "I know what a jolly responsive companion a doggie can be, but I've never been allowed to put a finger near Louis. You say he snaps at anyone except you and your maid, and you snatched him away from old Lady Peterby the other day, when she wanted to pet him, for fear he would bury his teeth in her. All that I ever see of him is the tip of his unhealthy-looking little nose peeping out from his basket or from your muff, and I occasionally hear his wheezy little bark when you take him for a walk up and down the corridor. You can't expect one to get extravagantly fond of a dog of that sort. One might as well work up an affection for the cuckoo in a cuckoo-clock."

"He loves me," said Lena, rising from the table, and bearing the shawl-swathed Louis in her arms. "He loves only me, and perhaps that is why I love him so much in return. I don't care what you say against him, I am not going to be separated from him. If you insist on going to Vienna you must go alone, as far as I am concerned. I think it would be much more sensible if you were to come to Brighton with Louis and me, but of course you must please yourself."

"You must get rid of that dog," said Strudwarden's sister when Lena had left the room; "it must be helped to some sudden and merciful end. Lena is merely making use of it as an instrument for getting her own way on dozens of occasions when she would otherwise be obliged to yield gracefully to your wishes or to the general convenience. I am convinced that she doesn't care a brass button about the animal itself. When her friends are buzzing round her at Brighton or anywhere else and the dog would be in the way, it has to spend whole days alone with the maid, but if you want Lena to go with you anywhere where she doesn't want to go instantly she trots out the excuse that she couldn't be separated from her dog. Have you ever come into a room unobserved and heard Lena talking to her beloved pet? I never have. I believe she only fusses over it when there's someone present to notice her."

"I don't mind admitting," said Strudwarden, "that I've dwelt more than once lately on the possibility of some fatal accident putting an end to Louis's existence. It's not very easy, though, to arrange a fatality for a creature that spends most of its time in a muff or asleep in a toy kennel. I don't think poison would be any good; it's obviously horribly over-fed, for I've seen Lena offer it dainties at table sometimes, but it never seems to eat them."

122

"Lena will be away at church on Wednesday morning," said Elsie Strudwarden reflectively; "she can't take Louis with her there, and she is going on to the Dellings for lunch. That will give you several hours in which to carry out your purpose. The maid will be flirting with the chauffeur most of the time, and, anyhow, I can manage to keep her out of the way on some pretext or other."

"That leaves the field clear," said Strudwarden, "but unfortunately my brain is equally a blank as far as any lethal project is concerned. The little beast is so monstrously inactive; I can't pretend that it leapt into the bath and drowned itself, or that it took on the butcher's mastiff in unequal combat and got chewed up. In what possible guise could death come to a confirmed basket-dweller? It would be too suspicious if we invented a Suffragette raid and pretended that they invaded Lena's boudoir and threw a brick at him. We should have to do a lot of other damage as well, which would be rather a nuisance, and the servants would think it odd that they had seen nothing of the invaders."

"I have an idea," said Elsie; "get a box with an air-tight lid, and bore a small hole in it, just big enough to let in an india-rubber tube. Pop Louis, kennel and all, into the box, shut it down, and put the other end of the tube over the gas-bracket. There you have a perfect lethal chamber. You can stand the kennel at the open window afterwards, to get rid of the smell of the gas, and all that Lena will find when she comes home late in the afternoon will be a placidly defunct Louis."

"Novels have been written about women like you," said Strudwarden; "you have a perfectly criminal mind. Let's come and look for a box."

Two mornings later the conspirators stood gazing guiltily at a stout square box, connected with the gas-bracket by a length of india-rubber tubing.

"Not a sound," said Elsie; "he never stirred; it must have been quite painless. All the same I feel rather horrid now it's done."

"The ghastly part has to come," said Strudwarden, turning off the gas. "We'll lift the lid slowly, and let the gas out by degrees. Swing the door to and fro to send a draught through the room." Some minutes later, when the fumes had rushed off, he stooped down and lifted out the little kennel with its grim burden. Elsie gave an exclamation of terror. Louis sat at the door of his dwelling, head erect and ears pricked, as coldly and defiantly inert as when they had put him into his execution chamber. Strudwarden dropped the kennel with a jerk, and stared for a long moment at the miracle-dog; then he went into a peal of chattering laughter.

It was certainly a wonderful imitation of a truculent-looking toy Pomeranian, and the apparatus that gave forth a wheezy bark when you pressed it had helped the pretence that Lena, and Lena's maid, had foisted on the household. For a woman who disliked animals, but liked getting her own way under a halo of unselfishness, Mrs Strudwarden had managed rather well.

"Louis is dead," was the curt information that greeted Lena on her return from her luncheon party.

"Louis dead!" she exclaimed.

"Yes, he flew at the butcher-boy and bit him, and he bit me too, when I tried to get him off, so I had to have him destroyed. You warned me that he snapped, but you didn't tell me that he was down-right dangerous. I shall have to pay the boy something heavy by way of compensation, so you will have to go without those buckles that you wanted to have for Easter; also I shall have to go to Vienna to consult Dr Schroeder, who is a specialist on dogbites, and you will have to come too. I have sent what remains of Louis to Rowland Ward to be stuffed; that will be my Easter gift to you instead of the buckles. For Heaven's sake, Lena, weep, if you really feel it so much; anything would be better than standing there staring as if you thought I had lost my reason."

Lena Strudwarden did not weep, but her attempt at laughing was an unmistakable failure.

THE HORSE THAT KNEW IT
WAS FRIDAY

Evelyn Smith

Phyllis and Richard Caldicott liked all the horses that came
with the carts, but best of all they liked Mr Campin the
milkman's. He was a dapple-grey, and when the sun was on his
back it shone as if he had been polished up, together with the
brass fittings on his harness, the brass axle-trees of the wheels,
and the big cans with taps at the back of the cart. And he was a
clever horse, knowing when to move from one house to
another, how long it took to measure out a pint and a half, and
a quart, and where Mr Campin liked to stop for a bit of gossip.

"I believe he likes to hear what's going on himself," said
Phyllis. "I believe he understands everything people say."

"Ah yes, 'e knows," said Mr Campin. "Dapple knows."

"Do you know me, Dapple?" said Richard, patting him.
"What's my name, then?"

"How could he say your name with that bit in his mouth?"
said Phyllis. "You're like the dentist when he asks if you've
been to many parties."

"Could he eat a lump of sugar with his bit?" asked Richard.

"You try 'im," said Mr Campin.

Phyllis had the lump, and she held it out, making her hand as
flat as could be in case Dapple should chew it by mistake, and
squeaking when she felt his big tongue curl over the sugar.

"Ah, 'e knows," said Mr Campin again. "Why, that 'orse
knows it's Friday."

"Can he say Monday, Tuesday, Wednesday, Thursday,
Friday?" asked Richard.

"Silly! Mr Campin doesn't mean like that," said Phyllis. "He
means he just knows, not that he talks about what he knows.
Don't you, Mr Campin?"

"That's about the way of it," said the milkman. And then
Dapple moved on to old Miss Lindsay's down the road. As the
cart went there, as to Dr Caldicott's, only on Friday, the day for

125

delivering eggs, it did seem as if Mr Campin might be right.

"I wish Father would get a horse instead of a car to take him on his rounds," said Richard.

"Yes. It must be lovely to do your work with a horse," said Phyllis. "Not a bit dull or lonely, always having him with you."

"I don't believe that horse knows it's Friday, all the same," said Richard. "I don't see how he could. It's just because he knows a good lot, that Mr Campin says he knows that too, so that he seems to be the wisest horse in the town."

"Well, it's no good talking about it, 'cause we'll never be sure," said Phyllis. "But I think he does, all the same."

Not many Fridays after this, the children went down to the garden gate, just after breakfast, to watch as usual for Mr Campin and Dapple. But there was no sign of them. Nine o'clock struck - half past nine. It was not a bad morning, and there seemed to be no reason for their not being in time.

"No eggs for you today, Emma?" shouted Richard, running round to the kitchen window. "Dapple isn't coming this morning."

"Well, I hope he is," said Emma. "Eggs I must have, even if I have to get them from the grocer's."

"Don't worry; Dapple will turn up," said Phyllis.

"No fear!" laughed Richard. "He's forgotten it's Friday."

But just at that minute came the rattle of wheels, and the smart clop-clop of Dapple's hoofs on the road. There was Dapple, and there was the cart, but no Mr Campin. The reins hung slack across Dapple's shining back; and he came up at a good pace, not as if he had been slowly walking from door to door. He stopped just where he always did on egg-delivery days, right in front of the brass plate on Dr Caldicott's garden wall.

"Where's Mr Campin?" Phyllis ran out and looked up and down the road.

"The eggs are here all right," said Richard, peeping behind

the cans and seeing the two brown baskets full of them. "Perhaps he wasn't able to come himself, so sent Dapple round to show us he really does know when it's Friday."

"I'm sure there's something wrong," said Phyllis. And she ran in to tell her father, and see what he said.

Dr Caldicott had not yet started on his rounds. Like Phyllis, he thought that some mishap must have befallen Mr Campin.

"Tell Wilson to wait with the car when he comes," he said to Emma. "We'll go back and see if anything has happened."

Emma lifted her eggs out of the cart, and Dr Caldicott jumped up to Mr Campin's place and took the reins, and Phyllis and Richard sat on the plank seat beside him. Dapple seemed rather in doubt as to whether he ought to go home before going on to Miss Lindsay's, but Dr Caldicott turned him, and off they went at a spanking pace, with the bells and ornaments on the harness jingling, and the milk-cans clanking merrily at the back. In quite a short time they were a couple of miles along the road, and then suddenly Dapple slackened pace. The children, leaning forward, gave a cry of horror as they saw poor Mr Campin huddled up at the side of the road. Dapple stopped.

"Keep calm. It's all right," said Dr Caldicott, jumping down from the cart and bending over Mr Campin. "He's alive and with all his wits about him. Aren't you, Campin?"

"Yes, sir, I'm alive right enough, but I can't move that leg, and as for my back ... I must say I'm glad to see you."

"Of course. Richard - up to that red house back in the fields over there as fast as you can, and see if you can get hold of a man to help me."

It was not long before poor Mr Campin was safely in bed, with his broken leg set. After delivering milk and eggs at the red house in the fields, early that morning, he had run across the lane to get into his cart, when a car had rushed round the sharp bend from the main road and knocked him, almost senseless, into the ditch. Early as it was, he had not expected other traffic in the lane, and evidently the driver of the car had not either - not did he seem to know or care what he had done, for he had driven right on and left Mr Campin with no one to help him - no one except Dapple.

"I said to 'im, 'Go on, old chap, you know it's Friday. Go straight on to Dr Caldicott's; couldn't be a better place for you to call at just now.' And 'e gave his head a shake, and off 'e went at once, knowing as could be, and fetched you sir, just like a human being."

"There, you see!" said Phyllis to Richard when she heard the story. "Dapple does know when it's Friday."

"I wonder if he would have known he must come up and ring the bell, if we hadn't been watching for him," said Richard.

"Never mind about that. He's just perfect in every way as he is," said Phyllis.

And Mr Campin thought so too.

A DOMESTIC ANIMAL

Shimazaki Toson

Her first misfortune was at her birth; she came into the world with short grey hair, overhanging ears, and fox-like eyes. Every domestic animal has a certain quality which attracts to itself the friendly feeling of man. But she did not have it. Nothing in her appearance seemed to be favoured by man. She was entirely lacking in the usual qualifications of a domestic animal. Naturally she was deserted.

However, she was also a dog, an animal which cannot live by itself. She could not leave the hereditary habitat to be fed by people and then go back to the wild native place of her remote ancestors. She began to search after a suitable human house.

This troublesome being strayed to the state of Kin san, a planter, where the building of the new wood-roofed rent house was just finished. The house was built along the village road of Okubo. The floor was high and the ground was dry. Moreover, there was a narrow, dark unoccupied space at the foot of the fence between this house and the next, so that she could promptly hide herself in emergency. She lost no time in occupying this underground refuge.

The urgent necessity was to get food. There were two more rent houses on this estate, which made four with the farm-like main house where Kin san's family lived. These houses stood each against the other, and trees with graceful branches were between them. Her sharp nose taught her first the direction of the kitchen. As she was hungry, there was no time for choice. Peeled skins of fruits, cold, evil-smelling soup, corrupt remnants of dishes - she ate everything she could get. If these were not enough to satisfy her, she smelt around even the dust heap, and hunted as far as she could hunt. Some dirty socks were soaked in the bath beside the well. Gladly, she drank the water from the bath.

There was an old shed in the garden. She decided to rest there in the shade, stretching out her four legs on the ground, which was warmed by the sunshine through the leaves, she sighed or scratched her itchy spots. When it was evening she entered her underground retreat and lay down on the charcoal bags which were under the floor above. She also tried a large bath. Sometimes she crept as far as the passage under the kitchen door, and slept on the charcoals in the warm charcoal box. Thus she began her life.

Kin san's family, at this time, kept a black and white dog called Pochi. This lively Pochi was the only being who welcomed her. Pochi seemed to have a sociable nature; he approached her politely scratching the ground. She made her return greeting by shaking her dirty tail.

But Kin san and the others who lived on his estate did not receive her as Pochi did. "Isn't it a great loss to be ugly, even among the animals," remarked one. "I might keep her, if she were a bit better," said another. All this was meaningless to her, and she was called Pup by these people who did not know. Each of the four houses had an "aunt," which was the name given to the hostess of the family. Not only these aunts, but also their children, laughed at and hated her and burst out calling her "Pup, pup." As for the "uncles," they were more dreadful. They chased her and threw things at her - stones, clumps of clay, the iron firestick. Once a big club of the door guard was flung after her, and made a wound on her hind leg.

Gradually, she understood the human mind. The significant twist of the mouth, a gesture as if to pick up something, the shrugging of shoulders and the bitten lips - all sentiments expressed against her - showed to her the deep enmity of the hunter. One day she was almost driven to bay in Kin san's kitchen. Nobody knows how she was able to find the means of escape! People were crying: "Bring the rope - the rope, the rope!" She was desperate, and running through the garden, she went towards the hot-house; turning around the barn, she escaped to the fields, where the flowers were to be sold on fete days.

"Gone, at last!" said one of the uncles. "Isn't she a

troublesome thing?" replied Kin san, who laughed like a good-natured man. It was not only once or twice that she met such hard experiences. But she was not a dog to be crushed down by this kind of hardship. She would hunt around for food calmly, with the appearance of saying: "This is my territory." Boldly she stepped into the new kitchen of the rent house, or went up to the verandah with her dirty feet. She bit off the laces from the garden slippers, and played with the washing, smearing it with mud and dust. she had no regard for the human children. This family had a girl called Ko chan, who liked to come out to play in the yard, in big wooden clogs trailing on the ground. She chased this girl for fun. Sometimes, Ko chan would bring out a piece of tasty-looking cake and show it to her.

"Look here! Look here, Pup!"

Instantly she jumped at Ko chan.

"Oh, Pup is wicked, mamma!"

This was always Ko chan's cry for help. Then the aunt came hastily and called Ko chan.

"Run away, Ko chan, quick! Why do you wear such big clogs?" But this time poor Ko chan had nothing left. She had taken the cake from the crying Ko chan, thus securing the sweets which are eaten by man. At such time, she usually licked the top of her nose with her red tongue.

Nevertheless, there was no intention of good or evil in her actions. These words she heard from the uncles and aunts of the estate, but nothing about them was known to her. She had no understanding of the etiquette and civility created by man. She was only a dog. Whether her action was impolite or not, that was not a question. She was only a poor animal, acting according to its nature.

The cold, scanty, miserable winter passed while she suffered this "better go away" treatment. It was a wonder that she did not die from hunger. The begging priest who used to come to Okubo every morning said that even he did not get much. As to the humble woman who took a child with her, she was refused mostly by "no business," or "nothing doing." Even human beings were in a sad state. How, then, could they spare a bowl of their cold rice for this ignorant and useless animal, this embarrassing dog? She roamed on the snow in the far-off places, and ate everything, even the skins of oranges.

Meanwhile, the spring had come. And at the time when the frost began to melt she seemed to be quite grown up. All the dogs, from Kin san's Pochi to Kuro of the bathing house, Aka of the timber-dealer's, and the fearful big dog which was kept at the neighbouring planter's, gathered around her. Wherever she went, she was followed by two or three dogs. So a comfortable place like the shade of the garden shed was overflowing with deep groans of dogs that sounded as if they wished to whisper or to flatter.

An aunt who came to the well-side with a bucket in her hand, saw this sight.

"My!" she said. "Pup was a female dog! I never noticed that!" and the aunt of the rent house who happened to be there also said, "Neither did I."

And the two aunts laughed, greatly amused.

She ought to be banished. Such was the argument which was raised in the estate of Kin san. Among the members of the four families, however, the arguments raged between two parties, the uncles and the aunts. According to the point of view which was insisted upon by the aunts, it was now different. She was not in the condition she was formerly, and it would be too pitiful if she were to have a baby. As is expected of those with experience, the aunts were sympathetic, comparing her with themselves. That may be so, but how awful it would be if she gave birth to children! This was the opinion held by the uncles. Indeed, there was nobody who was not anxious about her future.

She did know anything about this.

Another day, a carriage stopped at the door of Kin san. There was something like a lidless box on this carriage, which was covered with a dirty straw mat. Her quick nose smelt out what was in the carriage.

Following after a policeman in uniform came a dubious looking man, who entered the house. But she was not roaming in such a dangerous place. Pochi, Kuro and the other dogs began to cry all at once. Now, uncles, aunts, and all people of the village came out.

"Dog hunter, mamma!"

Ko chan hid herself behind her mother.

People ran around the garden. Kin san's daughter whose daily duty it was to water the flowers, ran out to the street with a dipper in her hand. A middle school boy who was painting a water colour picture, followed them, flinging away his tripod.

"Thither she escaped, hither she ran!"

The confusion itself was very extraordinary.

"Surely, Pup is killed," Ko chan said, trembling.

At last, she has escaped. A man with a big oak club in his hand, shook his head to his companion. "No use, no use," the policeman said and laughed when he went out of the gate. With disappointed looks the two men drew away the empty carriage.

Anyway she had escaped with her life. And, by and by, her bosom became larger. Her eyes began to be shaded with the restless colour. Now she must guard not only herself, but also her children within her womb. Thus the pleasant shade of the shed was no more the place for security. Even when she was comfortably lying on the moist earth, breathing out her agony for a while, she stood up as soon as she saw the shadow of a man. She could not be negligent even for a moment. To her eyes, there was nothing as merciless and cruel as the human being.

But, in spite of her fear, she could not leave the human house. How at ease she would be if, like other animals, she could go to a distant forest and give birth amid the green trees and grasses! Thus it might seem to the on-looker but it was not so with her, she was unable to change her inherited nature.

It was just at the beginning of June that she finished her duty of motherhood. Four puppies appeared in the hot-house of Kin san. Two of them were beautiful piebald puppies like that of Pochi, one was entirely black, and the other was of ambiguous grey, very much like herself!

Ah, it was in the morning of her motherhood that she first saw the smiles of human beings. It was also in that morning of her motherhood that she first had nourishing food since her birth.

"Pup - come, come." Opening the paper screen of the kitchen, the aunt at Kin san's began to call her, as she has called her since that day.

RIDING OUT

Maupassant

They were poor and just managed to make do on the husband's meagre salary. Two children had been born to the marriage, and what at first were straitened circumstances had turned into genteel, covert, shameful poverty, the poverty of old aristocratic families which insist on keeping up their position in society come what may.

Hector de Gribelin had been brought up in the country, in the ancestral seat, by a tutor, an old man in holy orders. His family were not rich, but they got by and managed to maintain appearances.

When he was 20 a situation was found for him and he became a clerk in the Admiralty at an annual salary of fifteen hundred francs. It was a reef on which he had run aground as do any who are not trained at an early age for life's hard struggle, who see existence through a rosy cloud, fail to learn the necessary guile and resilience, or have not when very young acquired special skills or particular abilities or the determination and energy to fight: anyone who has not had a weapon or a tool thrust into his hand.

The first three years he worked in the office were appalling.

He had met up with a number of friends of the family, equally diehard and impoverished, who had grand addresses in the sad streets off the Faubourg Saint-Honore. He had made a circle of friends.

It was in these circles that Hector met and married a girl who was as poor and as well-born as he. They had two children in four years. Hard-pressed by poverty, the only amusements they could afford were walks along the Champs-Elysees on a Sunday and the occasional visit to the theatre once or twice a winter, which they were able to manage only because a colleague passed on complimentary tickets. But one spring, his superior chose Hector to undertake some additional work, and for it he received a special bonus of three hundred francs.

When he came home with the money, he said to his wife: "Henriette, my dear, we're going to give ourselves a bit of a treat. We could take the children somewhere nice."

They talked it over at length and finally decided that they would have lunch in the country.

Hector said: "We don't do this sort of thing every day of the week, so we'll hire an open coach for you, the children and the maid, and I'll get a horse from the riding school for me. It'll do me good."

For the rest of the week, all they talked about was the outing they had planned.

Every evening when he got back from the office, Hector picked up his oldest son, sat him astride his leg, and rocking him up and down as hard as he could, told him: "This is how Daddy'll be galloping on Sunday when we're riding out."

All day long, the little boy straddled chairs and rode them round the room shouting: "I'm like Daddy on the gee-gee!"

Even the maid looked wonderingly at her master at the thought of him riding alongside the coach on his horse. At mealtimes she listened to him holding forth about horsemanship and telling tales about his exploits in the old days, on his father's estate. If he did say it himself, he had been properly schooled: put a horse between his legs and he was fearless, quite fearless! Rubbing his hands together, he told his wife several times: if they give me a horse that's hard to handle, I'll be only too pleased. You'll be able to see how well I ride. If you like, we'll come back via the Champs-Elysees just when people are coming out of the Bois de Boulogne. We'll be cutting a bit of a dash, and I wouldn't be at all put out to bump into some of the chaps from the Ministry. It's the sort of thing that makes the top brass think better of you."

When the great day came, the coach and the horse arrived at the door together. He went down at once to take a look at his steed. He had had understraps sewn onto his trouser bottoms. He thwacked his leg with a riding-crop he had bought the day before.

He lifted and felt the horse's legs one by one, prodded its neck, flanks and hocks, probed its back with his fingers, opened its mouth, examining its teeth, said how old it was, and when his family came down, gave them a lecture on the theory and uses of the horse in general and on this horse in particular which he pronounced first-rate.

When everyone had been properly seated in the coach he checked the saddle straps. Then, putting one foot in the stirrup, he sat heavily on the horse which shied under the weight and almost unseated its rider.

Unnerved, Hector tried to soothe it: "Steady, boy, steady."

When the mount had regained its calm and the rider his composure, Hector asked: "Everybody ready?"

They all replied: "Yes!"

He gave the order: "Then away we go!"

The cavalcade moved off.

Every eye was on him. He rode English-style, rising excessively high in the saddle. He hardly waited to make contact with it before bouncing up as though launching himself into space. Several times he looked as though he would finish up on the horse's neck. He stared straight in front of him, his face very tense and pale.

His wife, who had one of the children on her knee while the maid held the other, kept saying: "Look at Daddy! Look at Daddy!"

Excited by the movement of the carriage, the thrill of it all and the wind in their faces, the two boys shouted shrilly until the horse, frightened by their cries, broke into gallop. While the rider was trying to rein him in, his hat fell to the ground. The coachman had to step down from his seat to pick it up, and as Hector was getting it back from him he called to his wife from a little way off: "Can't you stop the children shouting like that? You'll make him bolt and me with him."

With the provisions packed away in the boot of the carriage, they had a picnic lunch in the woods at Le Visinet.

Although the coachman saw to all three horses, Hector kept getting up and going over to see if his mount needed anything. He stroked its neck and gave it bread and cakes and sugar. He said, "he's a bit rough when he trots. He even shook me up a bit for the first couple of minutes. But you saw how quickly I got the hang of him: he learned who was master. He'll be as good as gold now."

They returned via the Champs-Elysses as planned.

The huge concourse swarmed with carriages. And on either side there were so many people strolling that they looked like two long black ribbons stretching from the Arc de Triomphe down to the Place de la Concorde. A burst of sunlight streamed down on the bustling throng and glinted in the varnished coachwork, the steel-studded harness, and the door-handles of the elegant barouches. The crowds of people, carriages, and horses seemed drunk with life and driven by some crazy urge to keep on the move. And at the far end, in the Place de la Concorde, the Obelisk rose up out of a golden haze.

As soon as Hector's horse had passed the Arc de Triomphe it seemed to get a new lease of life. It weaved through the traffic, at a fast trot and made for the stables in spite of all its rider's efforts to pacify it.

The coach had been left a long way behind now. When the horse was level with the Palais de L'Industrie, it saw a stretch of turf, veered to the right, and set off at a gallop.

An old woman in an apron was quietly crossing the road. She was right in the path of Hector who was bearing down on her like an express train. Unable to control his mount, he began shouting for all his worth: "Look out! Get out of the way!"

Perhaps she was deaf, for she carried blissfully on walking until the very last moment. Caught by the chest of the horse which was going flat out, she was bowled over and, three somersaults later, landed ten paces away with her skirts in the air.

There were shouts of "stop him!"

Hector, hanging on for dear life, clung to the horse's mane and yelled: "Help!" His steed gave a sickening lurch and he shot like a bullet between its ears into the arms of a policeman who had been running towards him.

Within seconds, an angry, vociferous, gesticulating mob had gathered round him. One old gentleman in particular, sporting a large round medal and a large white moustache, seemed quite beside himself: "Hell's teeth, man! You can't go round killing people in the streets just because you don't know how to handle a horse."

Then four men appeared carrying the old woman. She seemed to be dead. Her face was yellow, her hat was askew on her head, and she was covered in dust.

"Take her into the chemist's," the old gent barked. "We're going straight to the police station."

Hector was marched off, sandwiched between two policemen. A third led his horse. A crowd walked behind him and suddenly the open coach came into view. His wife leaped out, the maid had hysterics, and the children began to snivel. He explained that he was on his way home, that he had knocked a woman over, that everything was all right. His distracted family drove off.

At the police station matters proceeded quickly. He gave his name, Hector de Gribelin, an official at the Admiralty. But then they had to stand around waiting for news of the injured party. A policeman, who had been sent to make enquiries, returned saying that she had regained consciousness but was complaining of terrible internal pains. She was a charlady aged 65 and her name was Madame Simon.

When he heard that she was not dead, Hector breathed again and undertook to meet the cost of her full recovery. Then he hurried back to the chemist's shop.

A crowd had gathered outside the door. The old woman was sitting sprawling in a chair and moaning: her hands were lifeless and her face looked dazed. Two doctors were still examining her. There were no bones broken, but there were fears of internal lesions.

Hector spoke to her: "Are you in much pain?"

"Ooooh, I'll say."

"Where does it hurt?"

"It's like a burning I got in me innards." A doctor came up to him: "Are you the person who was responsible for causing the accident?"

"That's right."

"This woman needs proper medical attention. I know of a clinic which would look after her for six francs a day. Would you like me to arrange it?"

Hector jumped at the offer, thanked him, and went home much relieved.

His weeping wife was waiting for him: he allayed her fears.

"It's nothing. This Madame Simon person is already feeling a great deal better and she'll be quite over it in three days. I packed her off to a clinic. There's nothing to worry about."

Next day, after leaving the office, he went round to find out how Madame Simon was getting along. He found her drinking a dish of beef-tea with evident relish.

"Well, how do you feel?" he said.

She replied. "Just the same, kind of you to ask, I'm sure. Feeling pretty down. Can't say I'm much better."

The doctor said it was best to wait a while since there might be complications.

He let three days go by and then went back. The old woman, fresh complexioned and clear-eyed, began groaning as soon as she saw him: "Ain't got the strength to move me arms and legs, bless you. Weak as a kitten, I am. don't suppose I'll ever get over it, not till the day I die."

A shiver ran down Hector's back. He asked to see the doctor. The doctor raised his arms hopelessly.

"I'm afraid there's nothing I can do. I can't make it out. Every

140

time we try to lift her, she screams her head off. We can't even move the chair without her making the most awful racket. I must believe what she tells me. Only she knows how she feels. Until I see her walking, I cannot assume that she may be telling lies."

The old woman sat there listening, without moving and with a crafty look in her eye.

A week went by, then two, then a month. Madame Simon never left her chair. She ate from morning till night, grew fat, chatted happily with the other patients, and seemed accustomed to being immobile as though it were a well-earned rest for fifty years of traipsing up and down flights of stairs, turning mattresses, carrying coal from one floor to the next, sweeping and scrubbing.

A bemused Hector went to see her every day and every day he found her calm and serene and lamenting: "Can't move me arms or legs, bless you, jest can't."

Every evening, Mme de Gribelin, with lead in her heart, would ask: "How is Madame Simon?"

And each time she asked, he would reply desperately: "No change. Absolutely no change."

They dismissed their maid, for her wages were becoming a strain. They cut back even more and the bonus evaporated completely.

Finally Hector summoned four eminent doctors. They stood round the old woman. She let herself be examined, poked, and probed, but kept a beady eye on them all the time.

"We'll have to get her moving," said one.

"I can't, I tell you," she said. "Can't move a blessed thing." They took hold of her, stood her on her feet, and dragged her along for a few steps. But she slipped through their hands and fell in a heap on the floor screaming so terribly that they sat her down on her chair again with the utmost care.

The opinion they gave was inconclusive, though they did state that there was no question that the old woman could return to work.

When Hector gave his wife the news, she collapsed onto a chair and said brokenly: "It would be better if we had her to live here. It would be cheaper."

He gave a start: "Here? To live with us? You can't be serious!"

But resigned now to anything that might happen and with tears in her eyes, she replied: "I'm sorry dear. But it's not my fault ..."

GARM - A HOSTAGE

Rudyard Kipling

One night, a very long time ago, I drove to an Indian military cantonment called Mian Mir to see amateur theatricals. At the back of the Infantry barracks a soldier, his cap over one eye, rushed in front of the horses and shouted that he was a dangerous highway robber. As a matter of fact he was a friend of mine, so I told him to go home before anyone caught him; but he fell under the pole, and I heard voices of a military guard in search of someone.

The driver and I coaxed him into the carriage, drove home swiftly, undressed him and put him to bed, where he awoke next morning with a sore headache, very much ashamed. When his uniform was cleaned and dried, and he had been shaved and washed and made neat, I drove him back to barracks with his arm in a fine white sling, and reported that I had accidentally run over him. I did not tell this story to my friend's sergeant, who was a hostile and unbelieving person, but to his lieutenant, who did not know us quite so well.

Three days later my friend came to call, and at his heels slobbered and fawned one of the finest bull-terriers - of the old-fashioned breed, two parts bull and one terrier - that I had ever set eyes on. He was pure white, with a fawn-coloured saddle just behind his neck, and a fawn diamond at the root of his thin whippy tail. I had admired him distantly for more than a year; and Vixen, my own fox-terrier, knew him to, but did not approve.

"He's for you," said my friend; but he did not look as though he liked parting with him.

"Nonsense! That dog's worth more than most men, Stanley," I said.

"He's that and more. 'Tention!'"

The dog rose on his hind legs and stood upright for a full minute. "Eyes right!"

He sat on his haunches and turned his head sharp to the right. At a sign he rose and barked three times. Then he shook hands with his right paw and bounded lightly to my shoulder. Here he made himself into a necktie, limp and lifeless, hanging down on either side of my neck. I was told to pick him up and throw him in the air. He fell with a howl, and held up one leg.

"Part of the trick," said his owner. "You're going to die now. Dig yourself your little grave and shut your little eye."

Still limping, the dog hobbled to the garden-edge, dug a hole and lay down in it. When told that he was cured he jumped out, wagging his tail, and whining for applause. He was put through half a dozen tricks, such as showing how he would hold a man safe (I was that man, and he sat down before me, his teeth bared, ready to spring), and how he would stop eating at the word of command. I had no more than finished praising him when my friend made a gesture that stopped the dog as though he had been shot, took a piece of blue-ruled canteen-paper from his helmet, handed it to me and ran away, while the dog looked after him and howled. I read:

"Sir – I give you the dog because of what you got me out of. He is the best I know, for I made him myself, and he is as good as a man. Please do not give him too much to eat, and please do not give him back to me, for I'm not going to take him, if you will keep him. So please do not try to give him back any more. I have kept his name back, so you can call him anything and he will answer, but please do not give him back. He can kill a man as easy as anything, but please do not give him too much meat. He knows more than a man."

Vixen sympathetically joined her shrill little yap to the bull-terrier's despairing cry, and I was annoyed, for I knew that a man who cares for dogs is one thing, but a man who loves one dog is quite another. Dogs are at the best no more than verminous vagrants, self-scratchers, foul feeders, and unclean by the law of Moses; but a dog with whom one lives alone for at least six months in the year; a free thing, tied to you so strictly by love that without you he will not stir or exercise; a patient, temperate, humorous, wise soul, who knows your moods before you know them yourself, is not a dog under any ruling.

I had Vixen, who was all my dog to me; and I felt what my friend must have felt, at tearing out his heart in this style and leaving it in my garden. However, the dog understood clearly enough that I was his master, and did not follow the soldier. As soon as he drew breath I made much of him, and Vixen, yelling with jealousy, flew at him. Had she been of his own sex, he might have cheered himself with a fight, but he only looked worriedly when she nipped his deep iron sides, laid his heavy head on my knee, and howled anew. I meant to dine at the Club that night, but as darkness drew in and the dog snuffed through the empty house like a child trying to recover from a fit of sobbing, I felt that I could not leave him to suffer his first evening alone. So we fed at home, Vixen on one side and the stranger-dog on the other; she watching his every mouthful, and saying explicitly what she thought of his table manners, which were much better than hers.

It was Vixen's custom, till the weather grew hot, to sleep in my bed, her head on the pillow like a Christian; and when morning came I would always find that the little thing had braced her feet against the wall and pushed me to the very edge of the bed. This night she hurried to bed purposefully, every hair up, one eye on the stranger, who had dropped on a mat in a helpless, hopeless sort of way, all four feet spread out, sighing heavily. She settled her head on the pillow several times, to show her little airs and graces, and struck up her usual whiney sing-song before sleep. The stranger-dog softly edged towards me. I put out my hand and he licked it. Instantly my wrist was between Vixen's teeth, and her warning aaarh! said as plainly as speech, that if I took any further notice of the stranger she would bite.

I caught her behind her fat neck with my left hand, shook her severely, and said: "Vixen, if you do that again you'll be put into the veranda. Now remember!"

She understood perfectly, but the minute I released her she

mouthed my right wrist once more, and waited with her ears back and all her body flattened, ready to bite. The big dog's tail thumped the floor in a humble and peace-making way.

I grabbed Vixen a second time, lifted her out of bed like a rabbit (she hated that and yelled), and, as I had promised, set her out in the veranda with the bats and the moonlight. At this she howled. Then she used coarse language - not to me, but to the bull-terrier - till she coughed with exhaustion. Then she ran round the house trying every door. Then she went off to the stables and barked as though someone were stealing the horses, which was an old trick of hers. At last she returned, and her snuffing yelp said, "I'll be good! Let me in and I'll be good!"

She was admitted and flew to her pillow. When she was quieted I whispered to the other dog, "You can lie on the foot of the bed." The bull jumped at once, and though I felt Vixen quiver with rage, she knew better than to protest. So we slept till the morning, and they had early breakfast with me, bite for bite, till the horse came round and we went for a ride. I don't think the bull had ever followed a horse before. He was wild with excitement, and Vixen as usual, squealed and scuttered and scooted, and took charge of the procession.

There was one corner of a village nearby, which we generally passed with caution, because all the yellow pariah-dogs of the place gathered about it. There were half-wild, starving beasts, and though utter cowards, yet where nine or ten of them get together they will mob and kill and eat an English dog. I kept a whip with a long lash for them. That morning they attacked Vixen, who perhaps of design, had moved from beyond my horse's shadow.

The bull terrier was ploughing along in the dust, fifty yards behind, rolling in his run, and smiling as bull-terriers will. I heard Vixen squeal; half a dozen of the curs closed in on her; a white streak came up behind me; a cloud of dust rose near Vixen, and when it cleared, I saw one tall pariah with his back broken, and the bull wrenching another to earth. Vixen retreated to the protection of my whip, and the bull padded back smiling more than ever, covered with the blood of his enemies. That decided me to call him 'Garm of the Bloody Breast,' who was a great person in his time or 'Garm' for short, so leaning forward, I told him what his temporary name would be. He looked up while I repeated it, and then raced away. I shouted 'Garm'! He stopped raced back and came up to ask my will.

Then I saw that my soldier friend was right, and that dog knew and was worth more than a man. At the end of the ride I gave an order which Vixen knew and hated: "Go away and get washed!" I said. Garm understood some part of it, and Vixen interpreted the rest, and the two trotted off together soberly. When I went to the back veranda Vixen had been washed snowy-white, and was very proud of herself, but the dog-boy would not touch Garm on any account unless I stood by. So I waited while he was being scrubbed, and Garm, with the soap creaming on the top of his broad head, looked at me to make sure that this was what I expected him to endure. He knew perfectly that the dog-boy was only obeying orders.

"Another time," I said to the dog-boy, "you will wash the great dog with Vixen when I send them home."

"Does he know?" said the dog-boy, who understood the ways of dogs.

"Garm," I said, "another time you will be washed with Vixen."

I knew that Garm understood. Indeed, next washing day, when Vixen as usual fled under my bed, Garm stared at the doubtful dog-boy in the veranda, stalked to the place where he had been washed last time, and stood rigid in the tub.

But the long days in my office tried him sorely. We three would drive off in the morning at half-past eight and come home at six or later. Vixen, knowing the routine of it, went to sleep under my table; but the confinement ate into Garm's soul. He generally sat on the veranda looking out on the Mall; and well I knew what he expected.

Sometimes a company of soldiers would move along on their way to the Fort, and Garm rolled forth to inspect them; or an officer in uniform entered into the office, and it was pitiful to see poor Garm's welcome to the cloth – not the man. He would leap at him, and sniff and bark joyously, then run to the door and back again. One afternoon I heard him bay with a full throat – a thing I had never heard before – and he disappeared. When I drove into my garden at the end of the day a soldier in white uniform scrambled over the wall at the far end, and the Garm that met me was a joyous dog. This happened twice or thrice a week for a month.

I pretended not to notice, but Garm knew and Vixen knew. He would glide homewards from the office about four o'clock, as though he were only going to look at the scenery, and this he did so quietly that but for Vixen I should not have noticed him. The jealous little dog under the table would give a sniff and a snort, just loud enough to call my attention to the flight. Garm might go out forty times in all the day and Vixen would never stir, but when he slunk off to see his true master in my garden she told me in her own tongue. That was the one sign she made to prove that Garm did not altogether belong to the family. They were the best of friends at all times, but, Vixen explained that I was never to forget Garm did not love me as she loved me.

I never expected it. The dog was not my dog – could never be my dog – and I knew he was as miserable as his master who tramped eight miles a day to see him. So it seemed to me that the sooner the two were reunited the better for all. One afternoon I sent Vixen home alone in the dog-cart (Garm had gone before), and rode over to cantonments to find another friend of mine, who was an Irish soldier and a great friend of the dog's master.

I explained the whole case, and wound up with: "And now Stanley's in my garden crying over his dog. Why doesn't he take him back? They're both unhappy."

"Unhappy! There's no sense in the little man any more. But 'tis his fit."

"What is his fit? He travels fifty miles a week to see the brute, and he pretends not to notice me when he sees me on the road; and I'm as unhappy as he is. Make him take the dog back."

"It's his penance he's set himself. I told him by way of a joke, after you'd run over him so convenient that night, when he was drunk – I said if he was a Catholic he'd do penance. Off he went with that fit in his little head and a dose of fever, and nothing would suit but giving you the dog as a hostage."

"Hostage for what? I don't want hostages from Stanley."

"For his good behaviour. He's keeping straight now, the way it's no pleasure to associate with him."

"Has he taken the pledge?"

"If it was only that I would not care. You can take the pledge for three months on and off. He says he'll never see the dog again, and so, mark you, he'll keep straight for evermore. You know his fits? Well, this is one of them. How's the dog taking it?"

"Like a man. He's the best dog in India. Can't you make Stanley take him back?"

"I can do no more than I have done. But you know his fits. He's just doing his penance. What will he do when he goes to the Hills? The doctor's put him on the list."

It is the custom in India to send a certain number of invalids from each regiment up to station in the Himalayas for the hot weather; and though the men ought to enjoy the cool and the comfort, they miss the society of the barracks down below, and do their best to come back or to avoid going. I felt that this move would bring matters to a head, so I left Terence hopefully, though he called after me –

"He won't take the dog, Sir. You can lay your month's pay on that. You know his fits."

I never pretended to understand Private Ortheris; and so I did the next best thing – I left him alone.

That summer the invalids of the regiment to which my friend belonged were ordered off to the Hills early, because the doctors thought marching in the cool of the day would do them good. Their route lay south to a place called Umballa, a hundred and twenty miles or more. Then they would turn east and march up into the hills to Kasauli or Dugshai or Subathoo. I dined with the officers the night before they left – they were marching at five in the morning. It was midnight when I drove into my garden and surprised a white figure flying over the wall.

"That man," said my butler, "has been her since nine, talking to that dog. He is quite mad. I did not tell him to go away because he has been here many times before, and because the dog-boy told me that if I told him to go away, the great dog would immediately slay me. He did not wish to speak to the Protector of the Poor, and he did not ask for anything to eat or drink."

"Kadir Buksh," said I, "that was well done, for the dog would surely have killed you. But I do not think the white soldier will come any more."

Garm slept badly that night and whimpered in his dreams. Once he sprang up with a clear, ringing bark, and I heard him wag his tail till it waked him and the bark died out in a howl. He had dreamed he was with his master again, and I nearly cried. It was all Stanley's silly fault.

The first halt which the detachment of invalids made was some miles from their barracks, on the Amritsar road, and then miles distant from my house. By a mere chance one of the officers drove back for another good dinner at the Club (cooking on the line of march is always bad), and there I met him. He was a particular friend of mine, and I knew that he knew how to love a dog properly. His pet was a big fat retriever who was going up to the Hills for his health, and, though it was still April, the round, brown brute puffed and panted in the Club veranda as though he would burst.

"It's amazing," said the officer, "what excuses these invalids of mine make to get back to barracks. There's a man in my company now asked me for leave to go back to cantonments to pay a debt he'd forgotten. I was so taken by the idea I let him go, and he jingled off in an ekka as pleased as Punch. Ten miles to pay a debt! Wonder what it was really?"

"If you'll drive me home I think I can show you," I said.

So we went over to my house in his dog-cart with the retriever; and on the way I told him the story of Garm.

"I was wondering where that brute had gone to. He's the best dog in the regiment," said my friend. "I offered the little fellow twenty rupees for him a month ago. But he's a hostage, you say, for Stanley's good conduct. Stanley's one of the best men I have – when he chooses."

"That's the reason why," I said. "A second rate man wouldn't have taken things to heart as he has done."

We drove in quietly at the far end of the garden, and crept round the house. There was a place close to the wall all grown about with tamarisk trees, where I knew Garm kept his bones. Even Vixen was not allowed to sit near it. In the full Indian moonlight I could see a white uniform bending over the dog. "Goodbye, old man," we could not help hearing Stanley's voice. "For Heaven's sake don't get bit and go mad by any measly pi-dog. But you can look after yourself, old man. You don't get drunk and run about hitting your friends. You takes your bones and you eats your biscuit, and you kills your enemy like a gentleman. I'm going away – don't howl – I'm going off to Kasauli where I won't see you no more."

I could hear him holding Garm's nose as the dog threw it up to the stars.

"You'll stay here and behave and I'll go away and try to behave, and I don't know how to leave you. I don't know –"

"I think this is damn' silly," said the officer, patting his foolish fussy old retriever. He called to the private, who leaped to his feet, marched forward, and saluted.

"You here?" said the officer, turning away his head.

"Yes, sir, but I'm just going back."

"I shall be leaving here at eleven in my cart. You come with me. I can't have sick men running about all over the place. Report yourself at eleven, here."

We did not say much when we went indoors, but the officer muttered and pulled his retriever's ears.

He was a disgraceful, overfed door-mat of a dog; and when he waddled off to my cookhouse to be fed, I had a brilliant idea.

At eleven o'clock that officer's dog was nowhere to be found, and you never heard such a fuss as his owner made. He called and shouted and grew angry, and hunted through my garden for half an hour.

Then I said: "He's sure to turn up in the morning. Send a man in by rail, and I'll find the beast and return him."

"Beast?" said the officer. "I value that dog considerably more than I value any man I know. It's all very fine for you to talk - your dog's here."

So she was - under my feet - and, had she been missing, food and wages would have stopped in my house till her return. But some people grow fond of dogs not worth a cut of the whip. My friend had to drive away at last with Stanley in the back-seat; and then the dog-boy said to me: "What kind of animal is Bullen Sahib's dog? Look at him!"

I went to the boy's hut, and the fat old reprobate was lying on a mat carefully chained up. He must have heard his master calling for twenty minutes, but had not even attempted to join him.

"He has no face," said the dog-boy scornfully. "He is a spaniel. He never tried to get that cloth off his jaws when his master called. Now Vixen-baba would have jumped through the window, and that Great Dog would have slain me with his muzzled mouth. It is true that there are many kinds of dogs."

Next evening who should turn up but Stanley. The officer

had sent him back fourteen miles by rail with a note begging me to return the retriever if I had found him, and if I had not, to offer huge rewards. The last train to camp left at half-past ten, and Stanley stayed till ten talking to Garm. I argued and entreated, and even threatened to shoot the bull-terrier, but the little man was as firm as a rock, though I gave him a good dinner and talked to him most severely. Garm knew as well as I that this was the last time he could hope to see his man, and followed Stanley like a shadow. The retriever said nothing, but licked his lips after his meal and waddled off without so much as saying 'Thank you' to the disgusted dog-boy.

So that last meeting was over and I felt as wretched as Garm, who moaned in his sleep all night. When we went to the office he found a place under the table close to Vixen, and dropped flat till it was time to go home. There was no more running out into the verandas, no slinking away for stolen talks with Stanley. As the weather grew warmer the dogs were forbidden to run beside the cart, but sat at my side on the seat, Vixen with her head under the crook of my left elbow, and Garm hugging the left handrail.

Here Vixen was ever in great form. She had to attend to all the moving traffic, such as bullock-carts that blocked the way, and camels, and led ponies; as well as to keep up her dignity when she passed low friends running in the dust. She never yapped for yapping's sake, but her shrill high bark was known all along the Mall, and other men's terriers ki-yied in reply, and bullock-drivers looked over their shoulders and gave us the road with a grin.

But Garm cared for none of these things. His big eyes were on the horizon and his terrible mouth was shut. There was another dog in the office who belonged to my chief. We called him 'Bob the Librarian,' because he always imagined rats behind the bookshelves, and in hunting for them would drag out half the old newspaper-files. Bob was a well-meaning idiot, but Garm did not encourage him. He would slide his head round the door, panting, 'Rats! Come along, Garm!" and Garm would shift one fore-paw over the other, and curl himself round, leaving Bob to whine at a most uninterested back. The office was nearly as cheerful as a tomb in those days.

Once, and only once, did I see Garm at all contented with his surroundings. He had gone for an unauthorised walk with Vixen early one Sunday morning, and a very young and foolish artillery man (his battery had just moved to that part of the world) tried to steal them both. Vixen, of course, knew better than to take food from soldiers, and besides, she had just finished her breakfast. So she trotted back with a large piece of the mutton that they issue to our troops, laid it down on my veranda, and looked up to see what I thought. I asked her where Garm was, and she ran in front of the horse to show me the way.

About a mile up the road we came across our artilleryman sitting very stiffly on the edge of a culvert with a greasy handkerchief on his knees. Garm was in front of him, looking rather pleased. When the man moved leg or hand, Garm bared his teeth in silence. A broken string hung from his collar, and the other half of it lay, all warm, in the artilleryman's still hand. He explained to me, keeping his eyes straight in front of him, that he had met this dog (he called him awful names) walking alone, and was going to take him to the Fort to be killed for a masterless pariah.

I said that Garm did not seem to me much of a pariah, but that he had better take him to the Fort if he thought best. He said he did not care to do so. I told him to go to the Fort alone. He said that he did not want to go at that hour, but would follow my advice as soon as I had called off the dog. I instructed Garm to take him to the Fort, and Garm marched him solemnly up to the gate, one mile and a half under the hot sun, and I told the quarter-guard what had happened; but the young artilleryman was more angry than was at all necessary when they began to laugh. Several regiments, he was told, had tried to steal Garm in their time.

That month the hot weather shut down in earnest, and the dogs slept in the bathroom on the cool wet bricks where the bath is placed. Every morning, as soon as the man filled my bath, the two jumped in, and every morning the man filled the bath a second time. I said to him that he might as well fill a small tub specially for the dogs. 'Nay," said he smiling, "it is not their custom. They would not understand. Besides, the big bath gives them more space."

The punkah-coolies who pull the punkahs day and night came to know Garm intimately. He noticed that when the swaying fan stopped I would call out to the coolie and bid him pull with a long stroke. If the man still slept I would wake him up. He discovered too, that it was a good thing to lie in the wave of air under the punkah. Maybe Stanley had taught him all about this in barracks. At any rate, when the punkah stopped, Garm would first growl and cock his eye at the rope, and if that did not wake the man - it nearly always did - he would tiptoe forth and talk in the sleeper's ear. Vixen was a clever little dog, but she could never connect the punkah and the coolie; so Garm gave me grateful hours of cool sleep. But he was utterly wretched - as miserable as a human being; and in his misery he clung so closely to me that other men noticed it, and were envious. If I moved from one room to another, Garm followed; if my pen stopped scratching, Garm's head was thrust into my hand; if I turned, half awake, on the pillow, Garm was up and at my side, for he knew that I was his only link with his master, and day and night, and night and day, his eyes asked one question - "When is this going to end?"

Living with the dog as I did, I never noticed that he was more than ordinarily upset by the hot weather, till one day at the Club a man said: "That dog of yours will die in a week or two. He's a shadow." Then I dosed Garm with iron and quinine, which he hated; and I felt very anxious. He lost his appetite, and

Vixen was allowed to eat his dinner under his eyes. Even that did not make him swallow, and we held a consultation on him, of the best man-doctor in the place; a lady-doctor, who cured the sick wives of kings; and the Deputy Inspector-General of the veterinary service of all India. They pounced upon his symptoms, and I told them his story, and Garm lay on a sofa licking my hand.

"He's dying of a broken heart," said the lady-doctor suddenly.

"Upon my word," said the Deputy Inspector-General, "I believe Mrs Macrae is perfectly right - as usual."

The best man-doctor in the place wrote a prescription, and the veterinary Deputy Inspector-General went over it afterwards to be sure that the drugs were in the proper dog-proportions; and that was the first time in his life that our doctor ever allowed his prescriptions to be edited. It was a strong tonic, and it put the dear boy on his feet for a week or two; then he lost flesh again. I asked a man I knew to take him up to the Hills with him when he went, and the man came to the door with his kit packed on the top of the carriage. Garm took in the situation at one red glance. The hair rose along his back; he sat down in front of me and delivered the most awful growl I have ever heard in the jaws of a dog. I shouted to my friend to get away at once, and as soon as the carriage was out of the garden Garm laid his head on my knee and whined. So I knew his answer, and devoted myself to getting Stanley's address in the Hills.

My turn to go to the cool came late in August. We were allowed thirty days' holiday in a year, if no one fell sick, and we took it as we could be spared. My chief and Bob the Librarian had their holiday first, and when they were gone I made a calendar, as I always did, and hung it up at the head of my bed, tearing off one day at a time till they returned. Vixen had gone up to the Hills with me five times before; and she appreciated the cold and the damp and the beautiful wood fires there as much as I did.

"Garm," I said, "We are going back to Stanley at Kasauli. Kasauli - Stanley; Stanley - Kasauli." And I repeated it twenty times. It was not Kasauli really, but another place. Still I remembered what Stanley had said in my garden on the last night, and I dared not change the name. Then Garm began to tremble; then he barked; and then he leaped up at me, frisking and wagging his tail.

"Not now," I said, holding up my hand. "When I say, 'Go,' we'll go, Garm." I pulled out the little blanket coat and spiked collar that Vixen always wore up in the Hills, to protect her against sudden chills and thieving leopards, and I let the two smell them and talk it over. What they said of course I do not know, but it made a new dog of Garm. His eyes were bright; and he barked joyfully when I spoke to him. He ate his food, and he killed his rats for the next three weeks, and when he began to whine I had only to say "Stanley - Kasauli; Kasauli - Stanley," to wake him up. I wish I had thought of it before.

My chief came back, all brown with living in the open air, and very angry at finding it so hot in the Plains. That same afternoon we three and Kadir Buksh began to pack for our month's holiday, Vixen rolling in and out of the bullock-trunk twenty times a minute, and Garm grinning all over and thumping on the floor with his tail. Vixen knew the routine of travelling as well as she knew my office-work. She went to the station, singing songs, on the front seat of the carriage, while Garm sat with me. She hurried into the railway carriage, saw Kadir Buksh make up my bed for the night, got her drink of water, and curled up with her black-patch eye on the tumult of the platform. Garm followed her (the crowd gave him a lane all to himself) and sat down on the pillows with his eyes blazing, and his tail a haze behind him.

We came to Umballa in the hot misty dawn, four or five men, who had been working hard for eleven months, shouting for our daks - the two horse travelling carriages that were to take us to Kalka at the foot of the Hills. It was all new to Garm. He did not understand carriages where you lay at full length on your bedding, but Vixen knew and hopped into her place at once; Garm following. The Kalka Road, before the railway was built, was about forty-seven miles long, and the horses were changed every eight miles. Most of them jibbed, and kicked and plunged, but they had to go, and they went rather better than usual for Garm's deep bay in their rear.

There was a river to be forded, and four bullocks pulled the carriage, and Vixen stuck her head out of the sliding-door and nearly fell into the water while she gave directions. Garm was silent and curious, and rather needed reassuring about Stanley and Kasauli. So we rolled, barking and yelping, into Kalka for lunch, and Garm ate enough for two.

After Kalka the road wound among the hills, and we took a curricle with half broken ponies, which were changed every six miles. No one dreamed of a railroad to Simla in those days, for it was seven thousand feet up in the air. The road was more than fifty miles long, and the regulation pace was just as fast as the ponies could go. Here, again, Vixen led Garm from one carriage to the other; jumped into the back seat, and shouted. A cool breath from the snows met us about five miles out of Kalka, and she whined for her coat, wisely fearing a chill on the liver. I had had one made for Garm too, and as we climbed to the fresh breezes, I put it on, and Garm chewed it uncomprehendingly, but I think he was grateful.

"Hi-yi-yi-yi!" sang Vixen as we shot round the curves; "Toot-toot-toot!" went the driver's bugle at the dangerous places, and "Yow! Yow! Yow!" bayed Garm. Kadir Buksh sat on the front seat and smiled. Even he was glad to get away from the heat of the Plains that stewed in the haze behind us. Now and then we would meet a man we knew going down to his work again, and he would say: "What's it like below?" and I would shout: "Hotter than cinders. What's it like up above?" and he would shout back: "Just perfect!" and away we would go. Suddenly Kadir Buksh said, over his shoulder: "Here is Solon;" and Garm snored where he lay with his head on my knee. Solon is an unpleasant little cantonment, but it has the advantage of being cool and healthy. It is all bare and windy, and one generally stops at a rest-house near by for something to eat. I got out and took both dogs with me, while Kadir Buksh made tea. A soldier told us we would find Stanley 'out there,' nodding his head towards a bare, bleak hill.

When we climbed to the top we spied that very Stanley, who had given me all this trouble, sitting on a rock with his face in his hands and his overcoat hanging loose about him. I never saw anything so lonely and dejected in my life as this one little man, crumpled up and thinking, on the great grey hillside.

Here Garm left me.

He departed without a word, and so far as I could see, without moving his legs. He flew through the air bodily, and I heard the whack of him as he flung himself at Stanley, knocking the little man clean over. They rolled on the ground together, shouting, and yelping and hugging. I could not see which was dog and which was man, till Stanley got up and whimpered.

He told me that he had been suffering from fever at intervals, and was very weak. He looked all he said, but even while I watched, both man and dog plumped out to their natural sizes, precisely as dried apples swell in water. Garm was on his shoulder, and his breast and feet all at the same time, so that Stanley spoke all through a cloud of Garm - gulping, sobbing, slavering Garm. He did not say anything that I could understand, except that he had fancied he was going to die, but that now he was quite well, and that he was not going to give up Garm any more to anybody under the rank of Beelzebub.

Then he said he felt hungry, and thirsty, and happy.

We went down to tea at the rest-house, where Stanley stuffed himself with sardines and raspberry jam, and beer, and cold mutton and pickles, when Garm wasn't climbing over him; and then Vixen and I went on.

Garm saw how it was at once. He said goodbye to me three times, giving me both paws one after another, and leaping on to my shoulder. He further escorted us, singing Hosannas at the top of his voice, a mile down the road. Then he raced back to his own master.

Vixen never opened her mouth, but when the cold twilight came, and we could see the lights of Simla across the hills, she snuffled with her nose at the breast of my overcoat. I unbuttoned it, and tucked her inside. Then she gave a contented little sniff, and fell fast asleep, her head on my breast, till we bundled out at Simla, two of the four happiest people in all the world that night.

THEO AND HIS HORSES:
JANE, BETSY, AND BLANCHE

Theophile Gautier

After Theophile grew to be a man, he wrote a great many books, which are all delightful to read, and everybody bought them, and Theophile got rich and thought he might give himself a little carriage with two horses to draw it.

At first he fell in love with two dear little Shetland ponies who were so shaggy and hairy that they seemed all mane and tail, and whose eyes looked so affectionately at him, that he felt as if he should like to bring them into the drawing room instead of sending them to the stable. They were charming little creatures, not a bit shy, and they would come and poke their noses in Theo's pockets in search for sugar, which was always there. Indeed their only fault was, that they were so very, very small and that after all was not their fault. Still, they looked more suited to an English child of eight years old, or to Tom Thumb, than to a French gentleman of forty, not so thin as he once was, and as they all passed through the streets, everybody laughed, and drew pictures of them, and declared that Theo could easily have carried a pony on each arm and the carriage on his back.

Now Theophile did not mind being laughed at, but still he did not always want to be stared at all through the street, whenever he went out. So he sold his ponies and began to look out for something nearer his own size. After a short search he found two of a dapply grey colour, stout and strong, and as like each other as two peas, and he called them Jane and Betsy. But although, to look at, no one could ever tell one from the other, their characters were totally different, as Jane was very bold and spirited, and Betsy was terribly lazy. While Jane did all the pulling, Betsy was quite contented just to run by her side, without troubling herself in the least, and as was only natural, Jane did not think this at all fair and took a great dislike to Betsy, which Betsy heartily returned. At last matters became so bad that, in their efforts to get at each other, they half kicked the stable to pieces and would even rear themselves upon their hind legs in order to bite each other's faces. Theophile did all he could to make them friends, but nothing was of any use, and at last he was forced to sell Betsy. The horse he found to replace her was a shade lighter in colour, and therefore not quite so good a match, but luckily Jane took to her at once, and lost no time in doing the honours of the stable. Every day the affection between the two became greater: Jane would lay her head on Blanche's shoulder – she had been called Blanche because of her fair skin – and when they were turned out into the stable yard, after being rubbed down, they would play together like two kittens. If one was taken out alone, the other became sad and gloomy till the well-known tread of its friend's hoofs was heard from afar, when it would give a joyful neigh, which was instantly answered.

Never once was it necessary for the coachman to complain of any difficulty in harnessing them. They walked themselves into their proper places, and behaved in all ways as if they were well brought up, and ready to be friendly with everybody. They had all kinds of pretty little ways, and if they thought there was a chance of getting bread or sugar or melon rind, which they both loved, they would make themselves as caressing as a dog.

Nobody who has lived much with animals can doubt that they talk together in a language that man is too stupid to understand; or, if anyone had doubted it, they would soon have been convinced of the fact by the conduct of Jane and Blanche when in harness. When Jane first made Blanche's acquaintance she was afraid of nothing, but after they had been together a few months, her character gradually changed, and she had sudden panics and nervous fits, which puzzled her master greatly. The reason for this was that Blanche, who was very timid and easily frightened, passed most of the night telling Jane ghost stories, till poor Jane learnt to tremble at every sound. Often, when they were driving in the lonely alleys of the Bois

162

de Boulogne after dark, Blanche would come to a dead stop or shy to one side as if a ghost, which no one else could see, stood before her. She breathed loudly, trembled all over with fear, and broke out into a cold sweat. No efforts of Jane, strong though she was, could drag her along. The only way to move her was for the coachman to dismount, and to lead her, with his hand over her eyes for a few steps, till the vision seemed to have melted into air. In the end, these terrors affected Jane just as if Blanche, on reaching the stable, had told her some terrible story of what she had seen, and even her master had been known to confess that when, driving by moonlight down some dark road, where the trees cast strange shadows, Blanche would suddenly come to a dead halt and begin to tremble, he did not half like it himself.

With this one drawback, never were animals so charming to drive. If Theo held the reins, it was really only for the look of the thing, and not in the least because it was necessary. The smallest click of the tongue was enough to direct them, to quicken them, to make them go to the right or to the left, or even to stop them. They were so clever that in a very short time they had learned all their master's habits, and knew his daily haunts as well as he did himself. They would go of their own accord to the newspaper office, to the printing office, to the publisher's, to the Bois de Boulogne, to certain houses where he dined on certain days in the week so very punctually that it was quite provoking; and if it ever happened that Theo spent longer than usual at any particular place, they never failed to call his attention by loud neighs or by pawing the ground, sounds of which he quite well knew the meaning.

But alas, the time came when a Revolution broke out in Paris. People had no time to buy books or to read them; they were far too busy in building barricades across the streets, or in tearing up the paving stones to throw at each other. The newspaper in which Theo wrote, and which paid him enough money to keep his horses, did not appear any more, and sad though he was at parting, the poor man thought he was lucky to find someone to buy horses, carriage and harness, for a fourth part of their worth. Tears stood in his eyes as they were led away to their new stable; but he never forgot them, and they never forgot him. Sometimes, as he sat writing at his table, he would hear from afar a light quick step, and then a sudden stop under the windows.

And their old master would look up and sigh and say to himself, "Poor Jane, poor Blanche, I hope they are happy."

MORE FAITHFUL THAN FAVOURED

Miss Eleanor Sellar

There never was a more faithful watch-dog than the great big-limbed heavy-headed mastiff that guarded Sir Harry Lee's Manor House, Ditchley, in Oxfordshire. The sound of his deep growl was the terror of all the gipsies and vagrants in the county, and there was a superstition among the country people, that he was never known to sleep. Even if he was seen stretched out on the stone steps leading up to the front entrance of the house, with his massive head resting on his great fore-paws, at the sound of a footfall, however distant, his head would be raised, his ears fiercely cocked, and an ominous stiffening of the tail would warn a stranger that his movements were being closely watched, and that on the least suspicion or anything strange or abnormal in his behaviour he would be called to account by Leo. Strangely enough, the mastiff had never been a favourite of his master's. The fact that dogs of his breed are useless for purposes of sport, owing to their unwieldy size and defective sense of smell, had prevented Sir Harry from taking much notice of him. He looked upon the mastiff merely as a watch-dog. The dog would look after him, longing to be allowed to join him in his walk, or to follow him when he rode out, through the lanes and fields round his house, but poor Leo's affection received little encouragement. So long as he guarded the house faithfully by day and night that was all that was expected of him; and as in doing this he was only doing his duty, and fulfilling the purpose for which he was there, little notice was taken of him by any of the inmates of the house. His meals were supplied to him with unfailing regularity, for his services at insuring the safety of the house were fully recognised; but as Sir Harry had not shown him any signs of favour, the servants did not think fit to bestow unnecessary attention on him. So he lived his solitary neglected life, in summer and winter, by night and day, zealous in his master's interests, but earning little reward in the way of notice or affection.

One night, however, something occurred that suddenly altered the mastiff's position in the household, and from being a faithful slave, he all at once became the beloved friend and constant companion of Sir Harry Lee. It was in winter, and Sir Harry was going up to his bedroom as usual, about eleven o'clock. Great was his astonishment on opening the library door, to find the mastiff stretched in front of it. At sight of his master Leo rose, and, wagging his tail and rubbing his great head against Sir Harry's hand, he looked up at him as if anxious to attract his attention. With an impatient word Sir Harry turned away, and went up the oak-panelled staircase, Leo following closely behind him. When he reached his bedroom door, the dog tried to follow him into the room, and if Sir Harry had been a more observant man, he must have noticed a curious look of appeal in the dog's eyes, as he slammed the door in his face, ordering him in commanding tones to 'Go away!' an order which Leo did not obey. Curling himself up on the mat outside the door, he lay with his small deep-sunk eyes in eager watchfulness, fixed on the door, while his heavy tail from time to time beat an impatient tattoo upon the stone floor of the passage.

Antonio, the Italian valet, whom Sir Harry had brought home with him from his travels, and whom he trusted absolutely, was waiting for his master, and was engaged in spreading out his things on the dressing table.

"That dog is getting troublesome, Antonio," said Sir Harry. "I must speak to the keeper tomorrow, and tell him to chain him up at night outside the hall. I cannot have him disturbing me, prowling about the corridors and passages all night. See that you drive him away, when you go downstairs."

"Yes Signor," replied Antonio and began to help his master to undress. Then having put fresh logs of wood on the fire, he wished Sir Harry good night and left the room. Finding Leo outside the door, the valet whistled and called gently to him to follow; and, as the dog took no notice, he put out his hands to take hold of him by the collar. But a low growl and a sudden flash of the mastiff's teeth, warned the Italian of the danger of resorting to force. With a muttered curse he turned away, determined to try bribery where threats had failed. He thought that if he could secure a piece of raw meat from the kitchen, he would have no difficulty in inducing the dog to follow him to the lower regions of the house, where he could shut him up, and prevent him from further annoying his master.

Scarcely had Antonio's figure disappeared down the passage, when the mastiff began to whine in an uneasy manner, and to scratch against his master's door. Disturbed by the noise, and astonished that his faithful valet had disregarded his orders, Sir Harry got up and opened the door, on which the mastiff pushed past him into the room, with so resolute a movement that his master could not prevent his entrance. The instant he got into the room, the dog's uneasiness seemed to disappear. He stopped whining and made for the corner of the room where the bed stood in a deep alcove, and crouching down, he slunk beneath it, with an evident determination to pass the night there. Much astonished, Sir Harry was too sleepy to contest the point with the dog, and allowed him to remain under the bed, without making any further attempt to dislodge him from the strange and unfamiliar resting-place he had chosen.

When the valet returned shortly after with the piece of meat with which he hoped to tempt the mastiff downstairs, he found the mat deserted. He assumed that the dog had abandoned his caprice of being outside his master's door, and had taken himself off to his usual haunts in the basement rooms and passages of the house.

Whether from the unaccustomed presence of the dog in his room, or from some other cause, Sir Harry Lee was a long time in going to sleep that night. He heard the different clocks in the house strike midnight, and then one o'clock; and as he lay awake watching the flickering light of the fire playing on the old furniture and on the dark panels of the wainscot, he felt an increasing sense of irritation against the dog, whose low, regular breathing showed that he, at any rate, was sleeping soundly. Towards two in the morning Sir Harry must have fallen into a deep sleep, for he was quite unconscious of the sound of stealthy steps creeping along the stone corridor and pausing a moment on the mat outside his room. Then the handle of the door was softly turned, and the door itself, moving on its well-oiled hinges, was gently pushed inward. In another moment there was a tremendous scuffle beneath the bed, and with a great bound the mastiff flung himself on the intruder, and pinned him to the floor. Startled by the unexpected sounds, and thoroughly aroused, Sir Harry jumped up, and hastily lit a candle. Before him on the floor lay Antonio, with the mastiff standing over him, uttering his fierce growls and showing his teeth in a dangerous manner. Stealthily the Italian stole out his hand along the floor, to conceal something sharp and gleaming that had fallen from him, on the dog's unexpected onslaught, but a savage snarl from Leo warned him to keep perfectly still. Calling off the mastiff, who instantly obeyed the sound of his master's voice, though with bristling hair and stiffened tail he still kept his eyes fixed on the Italian, Sir Harry demanded from the valet the cause of his unexpected intrusion into his bedroom at that hour, and in that way. There was so much embarrassment and hesitation in Antonio's reply, that Sir Harry's suspicions were aroused. In the meantime the unusual sounds at that hour of the night had awakened the household. Servants came hurrying along the passage to their master's room. Confronted by so many witnesses, the Italian became terrified and abject, and stammered out such contradictory statements that it was impossible to get at the truth of his story, and Sir Harry saw that the only course open to him was to have the man examined and tried by the magistrate.

At the examination the wretched valet confessed that he had entered his master's room with the intention of murdering and robbing him, and had only been prevented by the unexpected attack of the mastiff.

Among the family pictures in the possession of the family of the Earls of Lichfield, the descendants of Sir Harry Lee, there is a full-length portrait of the knight with his hand on the head of the mastiff, and beneath this legend, 'More faithful than favoured.'

GREYFRIARS BOBBY An Extract

Eleanor Atkinson

This is a true story about a little dog called Bobby. He was a Skye Terrier, who loved his master, Auld Jock, dearly. When Auld Jock died Bobby would not leave his grave in Greyfriars Churchyard. People tried to take the little dog away and give him a home, but still he came back and lived in the churchyard, where his friends brought him food.

In no part of Edinburgh did summer come up earlier, or with more lavish bloom, than in old Greyfriars kirkyard. Sheltered on the north and east, it was open to the moist breezes of the southwest, and during all the lengthening afternoons the sun lay down its slope and warmed the rear windows of the overlooking tenements. Before the end of May the caretaker had much to do to keep the growth in order. Vines threatened to engulf the circling street of tombs in greenery and bloom, and grass to encroach on the flower pots.

Mistress Jeanie often brought out a little old milking-stool on balmy mornings, and sat with knitting or mending in one of the narrow aisles, to advise her man in small matters. Bobby trotted quietly about, sniffing at everything with the liveliest interest, head on this side or that, alertly. His business, learned in his first summer in Greyfriars, was to guard the nests of foolish skylarks, song-thrushes, redbreasts, and wrens that built low in lilac, laburnum and flowering current bushes, in crannies of wall and vault, and on the ground. It cannot but be a pleasant thing to be a wee young dog, full of life and good intentions, and to play one's dramatic part in making an old garden of souls tuneful with bird song. A cry of alarm from parent or nestling was answered instantly by the tiny, tousled policeman and there was a prowler the less, or a skulking cat was sent flying over tomb and wall.

His duty done, without noise or waste of energy, Bobby returned to lie in the sun on Auld Jock's grave. Over this beloved mound a coverlet of rustic turf had been spread as soon as the frost was out of the ground, and a bonny briar bush planted at the head. Then it bore nature's own tribute of flowers, for violets, buttercups, daisies, and clover blossoms opened there and later, a spike or so of wild foxglove and a knot of heather. Robin redbreasts and wrens foraged around Bobby, unafraid; swallows swooped down from their mud villages, under the dizzy dormers and gables, to flush the flies on his muzzle, and whole flocks of little blue titmice fluttered just overhead, in their rovings from holly and laurel to newly tasselled firs and yew-trees.

The click of the wicket gate was another sort of alarm altogether. At that the little dog slipped under the table-tomb and lay hidden there until any strange visitor had taken himself away. Except for two more forced returns and ingenious escapes from the sheep farm on the pentlands, Bobby had lived in the kirkyard undisturbed for six months. The caretaker had neither the heart to put him out nor the courage to face the minister and the kirk officers with a plea for him to remain. The little dog's presence there was known, apparently only to Mr Traill, to a few of the tenement dwellers, and to the Heriot boys. If his life was clandestine in a way, it was as regular of hour and duty and as well ordered as that of the garrison in the Castle.

When the time-gun boomed, Bobby was let out for his midday meal at Mr Traill's and for a noisy run about the neighbourhood to exercise his lungs and legs. On Wednesdays he haunted the Grassmarket, sniffing at horses, carts, and mired boots. Edinburgh had so many shaggy little Skye and Scotch terriers that one more could go about unremarked. Bobby returned to the kirkyard at his own good pleasure. In the evening he was given a supper of porridge, or milk at the kitchen door of the lodge, and the nights he spent on Auld Jock's grave. The morning drum and bugle woke him to the chase, and all his other hours were spent in close attendance on the labours of the caretaker. The click of the wicket gate was the signal for instant disappearance.

A scramble up the wall from Heriot's Hospital grounds, or the patter of bare feet on the gravel, however, was notice to come out and greet a friend. Bobby was host to the disinherited children of the tenements. Now, at the tap-tap-tapping of Tammy Barr's crutches, he scampered up the slope, and he suited his pace to the crippled boy's in coming down again. Tammy chose a heap of cut grass on which to sit enthroned and play king, a grand new crutch for a sceptre, and Bobby for a courtier. At command, the little dog rolled over and over, begged and walked on his hind legs. He even permitted a pair of thin little arms to come near to strangling him, in an excess of affection. Then he wagged his tail and lolled his tongue to show that he was friendly, and trotted away about his business. Tammy took an oat-cake from his pocket to nibble, and began a conversation with Mistress Jeanie. "I brought a picnic with me."

"Did you now? And how did you know about picnics, laddie?"

"Master Traill was telling Ailie and me. There's everything to make a picnic in the kirkyard. They couldn't make my legs good in the infirmary but I'm going to Heriot's. I'll just have to earn my living with my head, and not think about my legs. Isn't he a bonny doggie?"

"Aye, he's bonny. And you're a brave laddie not to fuss yourself about what can't be helped."

The wife took his ragged jacket and mended it, dropped a tear in an impossible hole, and a halfpenny in the one good pocket. And by and by the pale laddie slept there among the bright graves, in the sun. After another false alarm from the gate she asked her good man as she has asked many times before:

"What'll you do Jamie, when the minister finds out about Bobby, and calls you up before the kirk sessions for breaking the rule?"

We will cross the bridge when we come to the burn, woman," he invariably answered, with assumed unconcern. Well he knew that the bridge might be down and the stream in flood when he came to it. But Mr Traill was a member of Greyfriars auld kirk too, and a companion in guilt, and Mr Brown relied not a little on the landlord's fertile mind and daring tongue. And he relied on useful, well-behaving Bobby to plead his own cause. With all their caution, discovery was always imminent. The kirkyard was long and narrow and on rising levels, and it was cut almost across by the low mass of the two kirks, so that many things might be going on at one end that could not be seen from the other. On this Saturday noon, when the Heriot boys were let out for the half-holiday, Mr Brown kept an eye on them until those who lived outside had dispersed. When Mistress Jeanie tucked her knitting-needles in her belt, and went up to the lodge to put the dinner on, the caretaker went down towards Candlemaker Row to trim the grass about the martyrs' monument. Bobby dutifully trotted at his heels. Almost immediately a half-dozen laddies, led by Geordie Ross and Sandy McGregor, scaled the wall from Heriot grounds and stepped down into the kirkyard.

It was Sandy who presently whistled like a blackbird to attract the attention of Bobby. There were no blackbirds in the kirkyard, and Bobby understood the signal. He scampered up at once and dashed around the kirk, all excitement, for he had had many adventures with the Heriot boys at skating and hockey on Duddingston Loch in the winter, and tramps over the country and out to Leith harbour in the spring. The laddies prowled along the upper wall of the kirk, opened and shut the wicket, to give the caretaker the idea that they had come in decorously by the gate, and went down to ask him, with due respect and humility, if they could take Bobby out for the afternoon. They were going to mark the places where wild flowers might be had, to decorate 'Jinglin' Geordie's' portrait, statue, and tomb at the school on Founder's Day.

Mr Brown considered them with a glower that made the boys nudge each other knowingly. "Saturday isn't the day for him to be going about. He should have a washing and grooming to make him fit for the Sabbath, and by the look of you, you would be none the worse off for soap and water yourselves."

"We'll give him a washing and combing tonight," they volunteered eagerly. At that, annoyed by their persistence, Mr Brown denied authority.

"You know he isn't my dog. You'll have to go and ask Mr Traill. He's fair daft about the good-for-nothing tyke." This was understood as permission. As the boys ran up to the gate, with Bobby at their heels, Mr Brown called after them: "You bring him home with the sunset bugle and don't teach him any of your unmannerly ways or I'll take a stick to you."

When they returned to Mr Traill's place at two o'clock the landlord stood in shirt-sleeves and apron in the open doorway with Bobby, the little dog gripping a mutton shank in his mouth.

"Bobby must take his bone down first and hide it away. The Sabbath in a kirkyard is a dull day for a wee dog." The landlord sighed in open envy when the laddies and the little dog tumbled down the Row to the Grassmarket on their gypsying.

Straight down the length of the empty market the laddies ran, through the crooked fascinating haunt of horses and jockeys in the street of King's Stables, then northward along the fronts of quaint little handicraft shops that skirted Castle Crag. By turning westward into Queensferry Street a very few minutes would have brought them to a bit of buried country. But every expedition of Edinburgh lads of spirit of that day was properly begun with challenges to scale Castle Rock from the valley park of Princes Street Gardens on the north.

"I dare you to go up!" was all that was necessary to set any group of youngsters to scaling the precipice. By every tree and ledge, by every cranny and point of rock, stoutly rooted hazel and thorn bush and clump of gorse, they climbed. These laddies went up a quarter or a third of the way to the grim ramparts and came cautiously down again. Bobby scrambled higher, tumbled back more recklessly and fell, head over heels and upside down, on the daisied turf. He righted himself at once, and yelped in sharp protest. Then he sniffed and busied himself with pretences, in the elaborate unconcern with which a little dog denies anything discreditable. There were legends of daring youth having climbed this fierce cliff and laying hands on the fortress wall, but Geordie expressed a popular feeling in declaring these tales all lies.

"No laddie could go all the way up and come down with his head not broken. Bobby couldn't do it and he's more like a wild fox than an ordinary dog. Now, we're the Light Brigade at Balaclava. Charge!"

The Crimean War was then a recent event. Heroes of Sebastopol answered the summons of drum and bugle in the Castle and fired the heart of Edinburgh youth. Cannon all around them, and 'theirs not to reason why,' this little band stormed out Queensferry Street and went down, hand under hand, into the fairy underworld of Leith Water.

All its short way down from the Pentlands to the sea, the Water of Leith was then a foaming little river of mills, twisting at the bottom of a gorge. One cliff-like wall or the other lay to the sun all day, so that the way was lined with a profusion of every wild thing that turns green and blooms in the Lowlands of Scotland. And it was filled to the brim with bird song and water babble.

The laddies waded along the shallow margin, walked on shelving sands of gold, and where the channel was filled, they clung to the rocks and picked their way along dripping ledges. Bobby missed no chance to swim. If he could scramble over rough ground like a squirrel or a fox, he could swim like an otter. Swept over the low dam at Dean village, where a cup-like valley was formed, he tumbled over and over in the spray and was all but drowned. As soon as he got his breath and his bearings he struck out frantically for the bank, shook the foam from his eyes and ears, and barked indignantly at the saucy fall. The white miller in the doorway of the grey-stone, red-roofed mill laughed, and anxious children ran down from a knot of story-book cottages and dooryards.

"I'll give you ten shillings for the high-spirited dog," the miller shouted, above the clatter of the wheel and the swish of the dam.

"He isn't our dog," Geordie called back. "But he will not drown. He's got a good head on him and will not be such a little fool another time.

Indeed he had a good head on him! Bobby never needed a second lesson. At Silvermills and Canonmills he came out and trotted warily round the dam. Where the gorge widened to a valley towards the sea they all climbed up to Leith Walk, that ran to the harbour, and came out to a wonder-world of watercraft anchored in the Firth. Each boy picked out his ship to go adventuring.

They followed the leader along shore and boarded an abandoned and evil-smelling fishing-boat. There they ran up a ragged jacket for a black flag. But sailing a stranded craft palled presently.

Away they ran southward to find a castaway's shelter in a hollow on the golf links. Soon this was transformed into a wrecker's den, and then into the hiding-place of a harried Covenanter fleeing religious persecution. Daring things to do swarmed in upon their minds, for Edinburgh laddies live in a city of romantic history, of soldiers, of nearby mountains, and of sea-rovings. No adventure served them five minutes, and Bobby was in every one. Ah, lucky Bobby, to have such playfellows on a sunny afternoon and underfoot the open country!

And fortunate laddies to have such a merry rascal of a wee dog with them! To the mile they ran, Bobby went five, scampering in wide circles and barking and leaping at butterflies. He made a detour to the right to yelp saucily at the red-coated sentry who paced before the Gothic gateway to the deserted Palace of Holyrood, and as far to the left to harry the hoofs of a regiment of cavalry drilling before the barracks at Piers-Hill. He raced on ahead and swam out to scatter the fleet of swans sailing on the blue mirror of Duddingston Loch.

The tired boys lay blissfully up the sunny side of Arthur's Seat in a thicket of hazel while Geordie carried out a daring plan for which privacy was needed. Bobby was solemnly brought before a court on the charge of being a seditious minister and was required to take the oath of loyalty to English King and Church on pain of being hanged in the Grassmarket. The oath had been duly written out on paper and greased with mutton tallow to make it more palatable. Bobby licked that fat off with relish. Then he took the paper between his sharp little teeth and merrily tore it to shreds. And, having finished it, he barked cheerful defiance at the court. The lads came near rolling down the slope with laughter, and they gave three cheers for the little hero. Sandy remarked, "You wouldn't think such a great doggie would be living in the murky old kirkyard." Bobby had learned the lay of the tipped-up and scooped-out and jumbled old town, and he led the way homeward along the southern outskirts of the city. He turned up Nicolson Street, that ran northward, past the University and the old Infirmary. To get into Greyfriars Place from the east at that time one had to descend to the Cowgate and climb out again. Bobby dared down the first of the narrow lanes.

Suddenly he turned round and round in bewilderment, then shot through a sculptured doorway, into a well-like court, and up a flight of stone stairs. The slamming of a shutter overhead shocked him to a standstill on the landing and sent him dropping slowly down again. Wht memories surged back to his little brain, what grief gripped his heart, as he stood trembling on a certain spot on the pavement where once a coffin had rested!

"What ails the little dog?" There was something here that sobered the thoughtless boys." "Come away, Bobby!"

At that he came obediently enough. But he trotted down the very middle of the lane, head and tail low, and turned unheeding into the Saturday evening roar of the Cowgate. He refused to follow them up the rise between St Magdalen's Chapel and the eastern parapet of the bridge, but kept to his way under the middle arch into the Grassmarket. By way of Candlemaker Row he gained the kirkyard gate, and when the wicket was opened he disappeared round the church. When Bobby failed to answer calls, Mr Brown grumbled, but went after him. The little dog submitted to his vigorous scrubbing and grooming, but he refused his supper. Without a look or a wag of the tail he was gone again.

"Now, what have you done to him? He's not like his old self."

They had done nothing, indeed. They could only relate Bobby's strange behaviour in College Wynd and the rest of the way home. Mistress Jeanie nodded her head with the wisdom of women that is of the heart.

"Eh Jamie, that would be where his master died six months ago." And having said it she slipped down the slope with her knitting and sat on the mound beside the mourning little dog.

When the awe-struck lads asked for the story Mr Brown shook his head. "You ask Master Traill. He knows about it; and he can talk like a book."

Before they left the kirkyard the laddies walked down to Auld Jock's grave and patted Bobby on the head, and then went away thoughtfully to their scattered homes.

As on that first morning when his grief was new, Bobby woke to a Calvinistic Sabbath. There were no rattling carts of hawkers crying their wares. Steeped in sunshine, the Castle loomed golden into the blue. Tenement dwellers slept late and then moved about quietly. Children with unwontedly clean faces came out to galleries and stairs to study their catechisms. Only the birds were unaware of the seventh day, and went about their melodious business; and flower buds opened to the sun.

In mid morning there suddenly broke on the sweet stillness that clamour of discordant bells that made the wayfarer in Edinburgh stop his ears. All the way from Leith Harbour to the Boroughmuir eight score of warring bells contended to be heard. Greyfriars alone was silent in that babblement, for it had lost tower and bell in an explosion of gunpowder. And when the din ceased at last there was a sound of military music. The castle gates swung wide, and a kilted regiment marched down High Street playing 'God Save the Queen.' When Bobby was in good spirits the marching music got into his legs and set him to dancing scandalously. The caretaker and his wifie always came round the kirk on pleasant mornings to see the bonny sight of the soldiers going to church.

To wee Bobby these good, comfortable, everyday friends of his must have seemed strange in their black garments and their serious Sunday faces. And, ah! the Sabbath must, indeed, have been a dull day to the little dog. He had learned that when the earliest comer clicked the wicket he must go under the table-tomb and console himself with the extra bone that Mr Traill never failed to remember. With an hour's respite for dinner at the lodge, between the morning and afternoon services, he lay there all day. The restaurant was closed, and there was no running about for good dogs. In the early dark of winter he could come out and trot quietly about the silent, deserted place.

As soon as the crocuses pushed their green noses through the earth in the spring the congregation began to linger among the graves, for to see an old burying-ground renew its life is a peculiar promise of the resurrection. By midsummer, visitors were coming from afar, some even from overseas, to read the quaint inscriptions on the old tombs, or to lay tributes of flowers on the graves of poets and religious heroes. It was not until the late end of such a day that Bobby could come out of hiding to stretch his cramped legs. Then it was that tenement children dropped from low windows, over the tombs, and ate their suppers of oat-cake there in the fading light.

When Mr Traill left the kirkyard in the bright evening of the last Sunday in May he stopped outside to wait for Dr Lee, the minister of Greyfriars auld kirk, who had been behind him to the gate. Now he was nowhere to be seen. With Bobby ever in the background of his mind, at such times of possible discovery, Mr Traill re-entered the kirkyard. The minister was sitting on the fallen slab, tall silk hat off, with Mr Brown standing beside him, uncovered and miserable of aspect, and Bobby looking up anxiously at this new element in his fate.

"Do you think it seemly for a dog to be living in the churchyard, Mr Brown?" The minister's voice was merely kind and inquiring but the caretaker was in fault and this good English was disconcerting. However, his conscience acquitted him of moral wrong, and his sturdy Scotch independence came to the rescue.

"If the little dog, isn't seemly, those cats are the devil's own children."

The minister lifted his hand in rebuke. "Remember the Sabbath Day. And I see no cats, Mr Brown."

"You won't see any as long as the wee doggie is living in the kirkyard. And the vermin have kept away for the first time since Queen Mary's day. And now there are more singing birds than for many a year."

Mr Traill had listened, unseen. Now he came forward with a challenge to put all but the routed caretaker at his ease.

"Doctor, I have a question to ask you. Which is more unseemly: a well-behaving little tyke in the kirkyard or a scandalous organ in the kirk?"

"Ah, Mr Traill, I'm afraid you're a sad, irreverent young dog yourself, sir." The minister broke into a genial laugh. "Man, you've spoiled a bit of fun I was having with Mr Brown, who takes his duties seriously." He sat looking down at the little dog until Bobby came up to him and stood confidingly under his caressing hand. Then he added: "I have suspected for some months that he was living in the churchyard. It is truly remarkable that an active, noisy little Skye could keep so still about it."

At that Mr Brown retreated to the martrys' monument to meditate on the unministerial behaviour of this minister and professor of Biblical criticism in the University. Mr Traill, however, sat himself down on the slab for a pleasant probing into the soul of this courageous minister, who had long been under fire for his innovations in the kirk services.

"I heard of Bobby first early in the winter, from a Bible-reader at the Medical Mission in the Cowgate, who saw the little dog's master buried. He sees many strange sad things in his work, but nothing ever shocked him so as the lonely death of that pious old shepherd in such a picturesque den of vice and misery."

"Aye, he went from my place, very ill, into the storm. I never knew where the old man died."

"The missionary returned to the churchyard to look for the dog that had refused to leave the grave. He concluded that Bobby had gone away to a new home and master, as most dogs do go sooner or later. Some weeks afterwards the minister of a small church in the hills inquired for him and insisted that he was still here. This last week, at the General Assembly, I heard of the wee Highlander from several sources. The tales of his escapes from the sheep-farm have grown into a sort of Odyssey of the Pentlands. I think perhaps, if you had not continued to feed him, Mr Traill, he might have remained at his old home."

"No, I don't think so, and I was not willing to risk the starvation of the bonny Highlander."

Until the stars came out Mr Traill sat there telling the story. At the mention of his master's name Bobby returned to the mound and stretched himself across it. "I will go before the kirk officers, Doctor Lee and take full responsibility. Mr Brown is not to blame. It would have taken a man with a heart of trap-rock to have turned the woeful little dog out."

"He is well cared for and is of a hardy breed, so he is not likely to suffer; but a dog, no more than a man, cannot live on bread alone. His heart hungers for love."

"Gosh!" cried Mr Brown. "Are you thinking he isn't getting it? Jeanie is fair daft about Bobby, and then there's the tenement children and the crippled laddie crying out to fondle him."

"Still it would be better if he belonged to one master. Everybody's dog is nobody's dog," the minister insisted. "I wish you could attach him to you, Mr Traill."

"Aye, it's a disappointment to me that he'll not stay with me. Perhaps in time –"

"It's no use at all," Mr Brown interrupted, and he related the incident of the evening before. "He's cheerful enough most of the time, and likes to be with the laddies as well as other dogs, but he isn't forgetting Auld Jock. The wee doggie came again to where his master died. Man, you never saw the like of it. The wifie found him flattened out on a furry door-mat and crying to break his heart."

"It's a remarkable story; and he's a beautiful little dog and a happy one." The minster stooped and patted Bobby, and he was thoughtful all the way to the gate.

"The matter need not be brought up in any formal way. I will speak to the elders and deacons about it privately, and refer those wanting details to you, Mr Traill. Mr Brown," he called to the caretaker who stood in the lodge door, "it cannot be pleasing to God to see the little creature restrained. Give Bobby his liberty on the Sabbath."